"Can I walk you to your car?"

Surprised, Caroline shook her head. "Thanks, but that's not necessary. The parking lot's right behind the building. I'm just going to set the night alarm, then head down the alley."

David gave the dim passage a quick look. "I'd feel better about it if you'd let me see you to your car. My mother always told me that a gentleman should never let a lady walk down a dark alley alone." His lips quirked into a grin.

David was a gentleman, no question about that, Caroline reflected. Even her mother would approve. Not that it mattered. It wasn't as if they were dating or anything.

But I wish we were.

The startling thought came to her unbidden. How could she think such a thing? This was the brother of the man she'd loved—and lost. The man she *still* loved. She wasn't interested in getting involved with any man, let alone David.

But she had to admit to herself that she found David's presence in the alley—and her life—comforting. He made her feel protected, cared for. And special somehow.

IRENE HANNON

is an award-wining author who has been a writer for as long as she can remember. She "officially" launched her career at the age of ten, when she was one of the winners in a "complete-the-story" contest conducted by a national children's magazine. More recently, Irene won the coveted RITA® Award for her Love Inspired book *Never Say Goodbye*. The RITA® Award, which is given annually by Romance Writers of America, is considered the "Oscar" of romance fiction. Irene, who spent many years in an executive corporate communications position with a Fortune 500 company, now devotes herself full-time to her writing career.

In her spare time, she enjoys performing in community musical theater productions, singing in the church choir, gardening, cooking and spending time with family and friends. She and her husband, Tom—an ordained cleric who juggles ecclesiastical duties with a career in international sales—make their home in Missouri.

Irene invites you to visit her Web site at www.irenehannon.com.

ALL OUR TOMORROWS

IRENE HANNON

Steeple
Hill®

Published by Steeple Hill Books™

STEEPLE HILL BOOKS

Steeple
Hill®

ISBN-13: 978-0-373-87381-4
ISBN-10:   0-373-87381-6

ALL OUR TOMORROWS

Copyright © 2006 by Irene Hannon

All rights reserved. Except for use in any review, the reproduction
or utilization of this work in whole or in part in any form by any
electronic, mechanical or other means, now known or hereafter
invented, including xerography, photocopying and recording, or in
any information storage or retrieval system, is forbidden without
the written permission of the editorial office, Steeple Hill Books,
233 Broadway, New York, NY 10279 U.S.A.

All characters in this book have no existence outside the imagination of
the author and have no relation whatsoever to anyone bearing the
same name or names. They are not even distantly inspired by any individual
known or unknown to the author, and all incidents are pure invention.

This edition published by arrangement with Steeple Hill Books.

® and TM are trademarks of Steeple Hill Books, used under license.
Trademarks indicated with ® are registered in the United States Patent
and Trademark Office, the Canadian Trade Marks Office and in other
countries.

www.SteepleHill.com

Printed in U.S.A.

He has made everything appropriate to its time.
—*Ecclesiastes* 3:11.

With thanks and gratitude to the Lord for the many blessings that have graced my life.

Chapter One

"**Y**ou'll never guess who I saw today."

Caroline reached for a roll and gave her mother a bemused glance. She never won at this game, which had become a standard part of their weekly dinner. Judy James knew more people than the President of the United States. Or so it seemed. "I haven't a clue, Mom."

"Guess anyway."

Instead of responding, Caroline popped a chunk of the crusty roll into her mouth, savoring the fresh-baked flavor. No question about it—her mom was a whiz in the kitchen, even if she did have a few idiosyncrasies. Like her penchant for outrageous hats. And her eclectic taste in decorating, thankfully confined to the family room, which had done time as a South Seas beach shack, a Japanese tea house and a Victorian parlor—to name but a few of its incarnations. In light of those eccentricities, Caroline supposed this silly guessing game was a tame aberration. And it was one she felt obliged to indulge, considering how much she owed her mother, who had been a rock during the difficult months when grief had darkened Caroline's world, blinding her to everything but pain and loss. She couldn't have made it through that tragic time without the support of the older woman sitting across from her.

"Okay. How about…Marlene Richards."

A thoughtful expression crossed Judy's face. "Goodness, I haven't had any news of Marlene in quite a while. Whatever made you think of her?"

"I reviewed an obit today for a Maureen Richards for the next edition of the paper. No relation, it turns out. But it made me think of Marlene. She was a good Sunday school teacher. A bit unconventional, but all the kids loved her. I wonder what ever happened to her?"

"When she retired, she went on a mission trip to Africa. Liked it so much, she stayed. Last I heard, she lived in a little village somewhere back in the bush and taught school."

At her mother's prompt and thorough response, Caroline smiled and shook her head. "How in the world do you do that?"

"What?"

"Keep tabs on so many people."

"I make it a point to stay connected. And speaking of staying connected…do you want to guess again?"

"Nope." Focusing her attention on the appetizing pot roast, Caroline cut a generous bite and speared it with her fork.

"All right. Then I'll tell you. David Sloan."

The hunger gnawing at Caroline's stomach suddenly

turned into an ache that spread to her heart, and her hand froze halfway to her mouth. "David Sloan?"

"Yes. Isn't that a strange coincidence? I was at the post office, and as I was leaving I must have dropped my scarf, because the next thing I knew this nice young man came up from behind and handed it to me. He looked familiar, but it took me a few seconds to place him. He didn't remember me, of course. We only met that one time, just for a few minutes and under such sad circumstances. But when I introduced myself, the oddest expression came over his face." Judy tilted her head in the manner of an inquisitive bird. "Kind of like the one on yours right now."

Caroline lowered her fork to her plate, the pot roast untouched. David Sloan. Her fiancé's brother—and the man who bore at least some measure of responsibility for his death. For a moment, the taste of resentment was sharp and bitter on her tongue, chasing away the fresh flavor of her mother's homemade roll. But then her conscience kicked in, dissipating her resentment with a reminder that she bore the lion's share of responsibility for the tragedy—and triggering a crushing, suffocating guilt that crashed over her like a powerful wave, rocking her world.

"Anyway, he took a new job and moved to St. Louis a couple of months ago. Still, it's a big city. Seems strange that I would run into him, doesn't it?" Judy prodded.

"Yes." Caroline could squeeze only one word past her tight throat. With a shaky hand, she reached for her glass of water and took a long, slow swallow, struggling to rein in her wayward emotions.

"I'm sorry, honey." Distress etched Judy's features as she studied her daughter's face. "I had no idea the mere mention of Michael's brother would upset you."

"I didn't, either." Denying the obvious would be foolish. Her mother knew her too well for that.

Reaching over, Judy patted her hand. "Well, we just won't talk anymore about it, then. Except I did promise him I'd give you his regards. Now that I've done that, tell me about your day. Any hot news at the *Chronicle?*"

Switching gears wasn't easy. But Caroline appreciated her mother's efforts to distract her. It was a technique that had helped keep her sane during those first few weeks after Michael's death, as her world disintegrated around her. So she tried to change focus. And prompted by Judy's interested questions, she was able to maintain the semblance of a conversation. As the meal ended, her mother even elicited a smile or two from her with an entertaining story about her latest passion—square dancing—and the lessons she was taking with Harold, her reluctant partner and steady beau.

"So I said to Harold, 'Just listen to the caller. He'll tell us what to do. It's like assembling that glider in my backyard. You just follow the directions and it all comes together.' And he says, 'I didn't read the instructions for the glider.'" Judy shook her head in exasperation. "Now I know why the thing seems a little lopsided. And why he ended up with all those leftover parts."

By the time Caroline left, with her almost untouched, foil-wrapped dinner and an extra piece of dessert in hand, she felt a bit more settled. But as she drove home through the dark streets of St. Louis, a shiver ran through her—one that she knew was prompted by more than the damp cold on this rainy March night.

Although her numbing, debilitating grief had ebbed over time, the mention of Michael's brother had dredged it up from the deep recesses of her heart. Along with all the other emotions she'd wrestled into submission these past two years. Guilt. Anger. Blame. Resentment. Some of those feelings were directed at her; others, at David Sloan. But none of them were healthy. As a result, she'd tried her best to suppress them and to move on with her life. Yet it took only the merest incident, like the passing reference to David tonight, to remind her that they hadn't been tamed, just subdued.

The rain intensified, obscuring her vision, and she flicked on her wipers. With one sweep, they brushed aside the raindrops, giving her a clear view of the road ahead. Too bad she couldn't banish the muddled emotions in her heart with the same ease. But they clung with a tenacity that rivaled the ivy creeping up the side of her mother's brick bungalow, imbedding itself with roots that sought— and penetrated—even the tiniest crack.

As she pulled into her parking spot, the light in the front window of her condo welcomed her with its golden warmth and promise of haven. Set on a timer, it came on faithfully every day at five o'clock, lessening the gloom of coming home to a dark, empty apartment. It might be a poor substitute for the warm embrace of the man she'd loved, but that glow buoyed her spirits, which had a tendency to droop after she left the office. Her hectic days at the newspaper kept her too busy to dwell on her personal life during working hours, but it was harder to keep thoughts of the past at bay when she was alone.

It was getting easier, though. Each day, in tiny increments, the past receded a little bit more. It had been months since she'd had to pull the car over because her hands had begun to shake. She didn't choke up anymore when she heard a song on the radio that reminded her of Michael. She didn't cry herself to sleep every night. And, once in a while, a whole day passed when she didn't think about what might have been. That was progress.

She knew Michael would have wanted her to move on. He, of all people, with his love of life and live-for-today attitude, would have been the first to tell her to get over it and get on with her life. To live, to love and to laugh. To make every day count.

Caroline was doing her best to put that philosophy into action. But it didn't take much—as tonight's brief conversation proved—to remind her that she still had a long way to go before she reached that ideal.

And to make her wonder if she ever would.

David Sloan angled into a parking place, set the brake and rested his hands on the steering wheel as he read the sign a few doors down. *County Chronicle.*

A wave of doubt swept over him, and he hesitated. Was he making a mistake coming here? He hadn't seen Caroline since Michael's funeral, and her attitude toward him then had been chilly at best. Not that he'd blamed her. If he and Michael hadn't argued, Michael would have been more focused when he'd gone to meet that contact in the marketplace. His brother had always had great instincts. That was why he'd been such a successful photojournalist, why he'd risen through the ranks of the Associated Press to be one of their top shooters. It was why they'd sent him to the Middle East, knowing that he'd be able to get into the thick of things, make great images and emerge unscathed. Until that fateful day in the marketplace, when he had no doubt been distracted by their argument, and by concerns for their mother. So David understood why Caroline would blame him for Michael's death. For turning her world upside down. For destroying a man they'd both loved in the prime of his life. He blamed himself, too.

For almost two years he'd grappled with his complicity. But finally he'd come to terms with it—at least as well as he would ever be able to, he suspected. And some good had come out of his struggle, too. After much prayer, he'd reevaluated his life and made some dramatic changes, following a new path the Lord had revealed to him. The work he was doing now might not offer him the kind of income provided by the high-stakes mergers and acquisitions he'd brokered in his previous job, but it paid dividends in human terms. And even though it had been hard for David to let go of the financial security his former position had offered, he'd put his trust in the Lord three months ago and made the change. So far, he hadn't had a single regret.

But he had plenty of regrets about his role in Michael's death. And one of them involved Caroline. He'd always felt the need to contact her, to express his sorrow, to apologize. Though they'd sat side by side at Michael's funeral, her grief had been too thick for words to penetrate. When he had reached out a tentative, comforting hand to her once during those terrible few days, she'd recoiled, staring at him with a look of such profound loss and resentment that it was still seared in his memory. That was the main reason he'd never tried to contact her. Not the only one, but the main one.

As for the other reason…he wasn't going to go there. Until yesterday, it had been irrelevant, since he'd never expected to see her again. Yet the chance meeting with her mother, and the medallion resting in the inside pocket of his suit jacket, its weight pressing against his heart, had prodded him to do what he should have done months before. If she brushed him aside, so be it. He still had to make the effort to reach out to her and apologize. And then he would move on—and do his best to forget about her.

From the outside, the *County Chronicle* looked like any other storefront on the busy Kirkwood street, which still retained a small-town flavor even though it was a close-in suburb of St. Louis. On his way to the front door, he passed Dubrov's Bakery, Andrea's card shop and Fitzgerald's Café, all of which seemed to be family operations instead of the chain stores that were multiplying like rabbits around the country. He liked that. Liked the notion that even in this modern age of megastores and conglomerates—many of which he'd helped to create in his previous job—the entrepreneurial spirit continued to flourish. That people with enough drive and determination could still create a successful business to pass down to the next generation.

As he stepped into the lobby of the *Chronicle,* David

tried to calm his erratic pulse. The first moments would be awkward, at best. *Please, Lord, help me find the words to make the apology I came here to offer,* he prayed.

"May I help you, sir?" A dark-haired woman, who looked to be in her early thirties, spoke to him from behind a desk. Her nameplate identified her as Mary Ramirez, receptionist.

"Yes. Is Caroline James in?"

"Do you have an appointment?"

"No. I just took a chance she might be available. I only need a few minutes."

"May I tell her what this is about?" The woman reached for the phone.

"I'm an old…acquaintance. She'll know the name. David Sloan."

The woman didn't look convinced, but she punched in some numbers, anyway. "She's got a very full schedule. I'm not sure she'll be able to see you."

Caroline's mother had told him that she was the managing editor of the paper, so he was sure she was busy. And perhaps not inclined to mix professional and personal business. But since she didn't have a listed phone number—he'd checked that first—he hoped she'd give him a few minutes at the office.

"Caroline, it's Mary. There's a David Sloan here who would like to see you." After several seconds of silence, the receptionist spoke again. "Caroline? Are you still there?"

Shock. That had to account for Caroline's delayed response, David reasoned. Which did not bode well for the reception he was going to get—if he got one at all.

"All right." The woman was speaking again. "Yes, I'll let him know." She hung up and gave David a speculative look. "She'll be out in a sec. Have a seat while you wait." She gestured to a small grouping of furniture with a coffee table in the middle.

Relieved, David nodded and moved to one of the modernistic upholstered chairs. He didn't feel like sitting, but pacing wasn't an option, either. The receptionist was already casting discreet, but interested, glances his way. He didn't want to arouse any more curiosity than necessary. With studied casualness, he sat in one of the chairs, reached for a copy of the newspaper from among those fanned on the coffee table, leaned back and pretended to read the blur of words on the page in front of him. He was more nervous about this encounter than any of the high-powered, deal-making sessions he'd once participated in, when hundreds of millions of dollars had sometimes hung in the balance. Maybe because the capital here was emotional, not monetary. And for another reason he didn't want to consider.

As the minutes ticked by, David grew more apprehensive. What if Caroline had changed her mind? What if she refused to see him? He'd get the medallion to her somehow, he vowed, find another way to apologize. Perhaps he'd resort to a letter. That would be easier than dealing with her face-to-face. But not as personal. Or as noble. Still, if she didn't come out, he'd have to conclude that she didn't want to see him, and he'd be left with no other option. It wasn't ideal, but he…

Suddenly, the door to the inner offices opened and Caroline stepped through. He set aside the newspaper and rose slowly, using the opportunity to do a quick assessment of the woman who stood before him.

She was still gorgeous, no question about it. Michael had always appreciated beautiful women. Just as it had the first time they'd met, David's heart tripped into double time. Caroline was model-tall, just three or four inches shorter than his own six-foot frame. And slender. Maybe too slender now, he corrected himself. A jade-green silk blouse was tucked into her pencil-slim black wool skirt, and a delicate gold necklace dipped into the hollow of her throat. She radiated the same style, class and poise he recalled from their first meeting, when Michael had brought her home for Christmas to introduce his fiancée to him and their mother. Now, as then, he was struck by her sleek, shimmery hair, which was the color of an autumn hillside—rich brown, laced with glints of gold, bronze and copper. She'd changed the style, though. He recalled her hair being shorter. Her new look was longer, just brushing her shoulders.

He noticed other new things, as well. Faint, parallel furrows in her brow. Fine lines at the corners of her eyes, and a deep, lingering sadness in their hazel depths. She'd also aged in some subtle way he couldn't quite identify. He knew she was a year younger than him. Michael had mentioned it once. And it wasn't that she looked older than her thirty-five years, exactly. It was just that there was a weariness in her eyes that hadn't been there before. A timeless, ancient expression not related to age, but to experience. The kind of look shared by people who'd seen too much, been through too much.

But at least the animosity he'd glimpsed at the funeral was gone. In its place was wariness.

As David stood there, Caroline looked him over as well, though she had a less vivid picture in her mind for comparison. The Christmas they'd come home to announce their engagement to both families, she'd been focused on Michael. And at the funeral, her grief had been so overwhelming that she'd been aware of David only on a peripheral level. In fact, she'd gone out of her way to avoid him as she'd tried to deal with the avalanche of shock, guilt and resentment that had buried her in a suffocating blackness.

But she had always recognized the distinct differences in the two brothers. David was a couple of inches shorter than Michael, and his hair was dark brown while Michael's had been sandy and sun-streaked. Their eyes also provided a contrast. Michael's had been a sparkling, vivid blue, while David's were quiet and deep brown. Just as their physical appearance differed, so, too, did their personalities. Michael had been an adventurous extrovert. David was a cautious introvert. Or at least that's how Michael had characterized him. He'd always referred to David, five years his junior, as his kid brother, and called him "the suit" in a good-natured way. He'd told Caroline that David was destined for the corporate world and power lunches, that one day he would be rich and famous while Michael continued to tilt at windmills. And that was just fine with Caroline. It was one of the things she'd loved about Michael. His absolute passion for truth and his zeal for his job were the first things she'd noticed about him. The world needed more people like him. Instead, it had one less. Thanks to her—and, to some degree, the man now looking at her from across the room.

Caroline had almost refused to see David. But what good would that have done? Any blame he bore for Michael's death was far less than her own, after all. And Michael wouldn't have wanted her to be unkind to David. Though the brothers had been estranged for several weeks prior to Michael's death, she knew that their break had weighed on his mind. Despite their difference of opinion on their mother's care, Michael had never stopped loving his kid brother. And she suspected the feeling was mutual. She was sorry they hadn't had a chance to resolve their dispute before Michael was killed.

But that was in the past. Right now, David was waiting for her to speak, and she forced herself to walk toward him. Michael would want her to be cordial, she knew. Still, she found the whole situation awkward. And unsettling. Not to mention painful.

"Hello, David." She held out her hand, and her fingers were engulfed in a warm, firm clasp.

"Hello, Caroline. Thank you for seeing me."

His voice sounded huskier than she remembered, and despite the almost palpable tension between them, he exuded a deep-seated, inner calmness that somehow eased her nerves. Yet another difference between the brothers, she mused. Michael's dynamic energy had infused those around him with excitement and enthusiasm. David, on the other hand, came across as calm, steady and in control. Someone who planned before plunging. Michael had always plunged first and planned on the fly. That spontaneity was one of the reasons he'd been so good at his job.

"I'm afraid I don't have much time," she told David.

"That's okay. I took a chance stopping by without warning. But after I ran into your mother yesterday, I decided I'd put this off long enough."

"Mom told me she saw you at the post office. How is your mother doing?"

"She died a year ago. The Alzheimer's progressed far more rapidly than anyone anticipated. And her heart just kept getting weaker."

Her query had been routine and mundane, and she'd expected the same kind of response. Instead, his reply shocked her. Sympathy replaced wariness in her eyes. "I'm so sorry."

"Thank you. It was a shock, but in many ways I'm glad God called her home. Alzheimer's is an awful disease. It robs people of everything that made them who they were. In the end, she didn't know me anymore, or remember anything about the past. The mother I knew had left months before her physical body stopped functioning."

So now David was alone. Michael had told her once that they had no other relatives. Both of their parents had been only children, and their father had died years before.

"I'm sorry," she repeated.

He lifted one shoulder. "I survived. My faith was a great comfort."

Another contrast between the two brothers, Caroline thought, recalling Michael's skeptical attitude toward religion in general. Though the brothers hadn't been raised in a household where faith played a central role, David had sought out the Lord as an adult. And the Christmas they'd met, Caroline had discovered that he'd found something that she had envied deep in her heart. An inner peace. A sense of greater purpose. Something to cling to through the turbulent seas of life. She'd wanted to question him about it, but the time hadn't been right then. Nor was it now. In ten minutes she was scheduled to do a phone interview with the mayor, and she needed to get focused.

"Well…I do have to get back to my desk. Was there something you wanted to talk about?" she asked when the silence between them lengthened.

With a jolt, David realized that she wasn't going to invite him to her office. Although Mary appeared to be busy, he suspected that she was tuned in to the conversation taking place only a few feet away, and what he had to say wasn't meant for public discussion. But he wasn't leaving without accomplishing the purpose of his visit.

"Is there somewhere private we could speak?" He lowered his voice and angled his body away from the receptionist.

After a brief hesitation, Caroline nodded. "But I have a phone interview to do in a few minutes."

"I'll be brief."

Without responding, she turned and led the way to the inner door, holding up an ID card to the scanner. The door responded with a click and she pulled it open.

The office was much more expansive than David expected. And far more modern than the quaint exterior of the building had suggested. The newsroom was quite large and honeycombed with dozens of cubicles. There was a hum of activity, and staff members stopped Caroline twice to ask her questions as she led the way through the maze.

When they reached her glass-enclosed office, she stepped aside and motioned him in, then followed and closed the door behind her.

"Busy place," he commented.

"And this is a quiet day. You should see it when things are really hopping." She moved to her chair, putting the desk between them.

"I guess I didn't realize that a smaller paper would be so…thriving."

"The *Chronicle* isn't small. It's the second-largest paper in the city, next to the *Post-Dispatch,* and we continue to acquire smaller community newspapers. But I don't need to tell you how mergers and acquisitions work. You deal with that every day."

"Not anymore." At her surprised look, he explained. "I took a new job a couple of months ago. As executive director of Uplink, an organization that pairs gifted high school students in problem environments with mentors for summer internships. That's why I moved to St. Louis. But it seems you've changed directions, too. I thought you'd be back at the Associated Press by now."

Her eyes went flat. "No. I've seen enough blood, sweat and tears to last a lifetime. This suits me just fine." She checked her watch, and he got the message.

"I know you're on a tight schedule, so I won't keep you." He reached into the pocket of his jacket and withdrew a small, tissue-wrapped object. "When I was packing for the move, I came across this among Michael's things. A few weeks after he…after the bombing…AP sent me some personal effects that had been returned by the authorities. I didn't give them more than a cursory look at the time. It was too hard." He stopped and cleared his throat. "I did notice this, but to be honest, I thought it had been sent to me by mistake, that it belonged to one of the other victims. It wasn't a symbol I would have associated with Michael. But when I was packing, I looked at it more closely and saw the initials. I think it must have been something you gave him. So I thought you should have it." He handed it across her desk, his lean, strong fingers brushing hers as she reached for it.

Curious, Caroline unwrapped the tissue. Nestled inside lay a small pewter anchor on a chain. As she stared at the medallion, the air rushed out of her lungs in a sudden whoosh. She groped for the edge of her desk, and for a brief second the room tilted. Then firm, steadying hands gripped her upper arms, and the world stabilized.

"Are you okay? Why don't you sit down for a minute?"

She drew in a ragged breath before she lifted her head. David's concerned face was just inches from hers as he leaned across her desk.

"I'm fine. It was just a…a shock." Nevertheless, she made a move to sit in her chair, not trusting her shaky legs to hold her up.

As David released her arms, he shoved one hand in the pocket of his slacks. "I was pretty sure the initials on the back were yours."

Turning the anchor over, she traced the familiar inscription with a gentle finger. CMJ to MWS.

"I gave this to Michael the Christmas we got engaged." Her voice was whisper-soft. "He always told me that I was his anchor. That whenever the world got too crazy, he would think about me, and then everything made sense again. That I kept him stable through the storms of life. After I gave this to him, he never took it off. He said it was his good luck charm."

Her voice choked on the last word, and David swallowed hard. No doubt they were sharing the same thought: that he hadn't been so lucky the day he'd gone to the marketplace.

"There's something I've been wanting to say to you for two years, Caroline. I'm sure you know that Michael and I argued about Mom the night before he was…before he died. And that our relationship had been strained for several weeks. You have every right to put at least some of the blame for his death on me. I know he was upset when we talked. And I'm sure he was distracted when he went out on that assignment the next day. I lived with the guilt for almost two years, and even though I found some measure of peace about it after a great deal of prayer, I suspect it will always be with me to some degree. I just want you to know how sorry I am. And that I hope you can find it in your heart someday to forgive me."

The regret and anguish on David's face mirrored that in her heart. Yet she knew hers was far more deserved. That she was even more culpable than the man across from her. No one else was aware of that, though. She'd never spoken to anyone of the part she had played in Michael's death. But now that she realized the depth of David's distress, had glimpsed the burden of pain that weighed down his heart as he shouldered all the blame, she couldn't in good conscience keep her role a secret from him. It wouldn't be honest. Or moral. She might not agree with the steps he'd taken, against Michael's wishes, to institutionalize their mother, but she couldn't let him continue to think that he alone was at fault for the tragedy.

Gripping the medallion in a tight fist, Caroline rose. When she spoke, her voice was taut with tension. "The guilt isn't all yours, David. Or even mostly yours."

"What do you mean?" He sent her a puzzled look.

She tried to swallow past the lump in her throat. "Michael shouldn't have been in the marketplace that day. It was supposed to be me. I was working on a hot story, but I got sick. He volunteered to meet my contact for me." Her face contorted with anguish, and when she continued her voice was a mere whisper. "I was the one who should have been killed by the suicide bomber."

A shock wave passed through David as he digested Caroline's revelation—and tried to comprehend its ramifications. Somewhere, in a far corner of his mind, he realized that her confession had absolved him from a portion of the blame for the tragedy, and he felt a subtle easing of the guilt that had burdened his heart for two years. But in the forefront of his consciousness was the realization that for those same two years the woman across from him had borne a burden even greater than his on her slender shoulders. The man she loved had done her a favor, had taken her place and he'd been killed. He'd thought his guilt had been wrenching. How much more intense it must have been for Caroline, who lived now because Michael had died.

The devastated look on her face bore that out and twisted his gut into a painful knot.

"I'm sorry, Caroline." The words were wholly inadequate, but he didn't know what else to say.

"I'm the one who's sorry," she whispered. "You have every right to hate me."

"How can I hate you for getting sick?"

"Because I shouldn't have let that stop me. I still should have gone. It was my responsibility, not Michael's."

"How sick were you?"

She shrugged. "Pretty sick. I had some weird virus."

"Did you have a fever?"

"Yes. A hundred and three."

"You needed to stay in bed."

"That's what Michael said."

"He was right."

"No." Her voice was resolute. "I should have gone."

"You'd have been killed."

"I know. But it *should* have been me." Her voice broke on the last word.

"Do you think that's what Michael would have wanted?"

David's quiet question startled her. And the answer was obvious. No, of course not. Given a choice between who would live and who would die, Michael would have taken her place in a heartbeat. But that was beside the point. She wouldn't have let him.

She shook her head. "Thanks for trying. And thank you for this." She cradled the medallion in her hand, fighting back tears. She hadn't cried at work in a long time. And she didn't intend to start now.

"Maybe God had other plans for you, Caroline. Maybe that's why He took Michael instead of you."

Jolted, she stared at him. That was a new thought. And a generous one, considering that she was the primary reason David had lost the brother he loved. But it wasn't one she put much stock in. She saw no greater purpose in her life than had been in Michael's, didn't think she had any more to contribute than he had. His work had been Pulitzer-prize quality. She was good at her job, but not as good as he had been. No, that explanation didn't hold up for her.

She was saved from having to respond by the jarring ring of the phone, reminding her that she had an interview to conduct. Even if talking with the mayor right now about the new zoning law was about as appealing as…playing her mother's guessing game.

"That must be your interview. I'll let myself out."

"Thank you for coming today," she said as she reached for the phone.

"It was long overdue."

As she put the phone to her ear, mouthed a greeting and waited to be connected to the mayor, she watched David make a quick exit, then weave through the newsroom toward the front door. When he reached it, he turned back. Their gazes connected, and held, for a brief second. But it was long enough for Caroline to sense that for David, their meeting today had provided a sense of closure. Then he lifted his hand and disappeared through the door. It shut behind him, with a symbolic sense of finality, giving her the distinct feeling that he had no intention of contacting her again. That his visit today had tied up the last loose end associated with Michael's death.

Caroline wished she could find that same sense of closure. That she, too, could shut the door on her past. But for her, the pain, the regret, the guilt, just wouldn't go away.

David, on the other hand, seemed to have found some sense of comfort, some relief, some absolution, in his faith. Not to mention a wellspring of charity. Instead of hating her when she'd revealed her part in Michael's death—as he'd had every right to do—he'd put it in the hands of the Lord, suggesting that perhaps God had other plans for her.

And for just a moment, as she had on that Christmas when they'd met, she envied him his bond with a greater power, which had given him answers and lightened his burdens while hers still weighed down her soul.

Chapter Two

❧

"That's good news on the funding front, Martin. Every donation helps. Thanks for the report." Chairman Mark Holton checked the agenda for the Uplink board meeting. "Looks like you're next, Allison. What's the latest on signing up mentoring organizations?"

"Good news there, too. Several more businesses have agreed to take on student interns over the summer. But a lot of the companies I contacted had never heard of Uplink. I think we need to find a way to generate some additional publicity."

"Point well taken." Mark surveyed the eight-member board, ending with David. "Any thoughts?"

"Well, after only a couple of months on the job, I have limited experience to draw on," David responded. "But I've run into the same issue with my outreach efforts at schools. Some of the administrators are familiar with the program, but most of the students aren't. It wouldn't hurt to have some coverage in the local media."

"I agree." Mark turned to Rachel Harris, the publicity chairperson. "Have we pitched any stories in the past few weeks?"

"No. Not since the *Post-Dispatch* did that piece last fall. It might not be a bad idea to contact the *Chronicle,* considering its wide reach. I can make a cold call, but if anyone has a connection there it would be helpful."

"I know the managing editor," David offered.

"Excellent." Mark jotted a few notes on a pad in front of him.

Now what had prompted him to blurt that out? David chided himself in dismay. He'd had no intention of contacting Caroline again after he walked out of her office a few days before.

"Could you make a call?" Mark asked. "Rachel can follow up, but it might help if you paved the way."

David wasn't so sure about that. But short of explaining his link to Caroline—which he didn't intend to do—he was left with no option but to agree. "Sure. I'll call her later this week."

"All right. Now why don't you bring us up-to-date on your outreach efforts at the schools."

As David gave them a quick overview of his busy schedule of visits to area high schools, he focused on a few institutions in the most troubled parts of the city, where he'd put a great deal of effort into recruiting participants. When he ticked off their names, a few board members shifted in their seats and exchanged uneasy glances.

"Is there a problem?" David asked.

"I think there's some concern about soliciting participants from those schools," Mark told him when no one else spoke. "Many of them have gang problems, and those students may not be the best representatives for our program right now. If any of them cause trouble at their assigned businesses, it could hinder our efforts."

"And if they succeed, it could help our cause."

"It's the *if* we're worried about."

"Let me make sure I understand the issue." David folded his hands on the table in front of him and leveled a direct gaze at the chairman. "I thought the mission of Uplink was to reach out to gifted students who were in environments that might sabotage their continued education. I was working on the assumption that our goal was to offer them an opportunity to develop their talents and encourage them to continue in school by giving them role models and experience in a real-world setting. To provide them with a taste of the kind of life they might have if they persevere despite the obstacles that their present situations might present. Is that correct?"

"Yes," Mark affirmed.

"Then we need to be aggressive in our recruiting or we'll fail."

"We'll also fail if we recruit students who cause problems with the participating businesses."

Stifling a frustrated sigh, David nodded. "Understood. But unless we offer this program to those who need it most, we're doing a disservice to our mission."

"David has a point." All heads swiveled toward Reverend Steve Dempsky, one of the charter board members. "If we play this too safe, the program loses its meaning. Let's not forget that we were heading in that direction under our former director. We brought

David in to give the program some punch, to make it more dynamic and cutting edge. I don't think we want to tie his hands at this point. We need to trust his judgment and have confidence he won't take undue risks that put Uplink in danger."

As the board digested the minister's comments, David sent him a grateful look. Steve had been his college roommate, and they'd never lost contact. In fact, Steve had been the one who'd told him about this job and recommended him to the board. He appreciated not only his friend's confidence, but also his willingness to put himself on the line over an issue that was stickier than David had expected.

"Your points are well-taken, Reverend." Mark turned to the other members of the board. "Do we need any further discussion on this?" When those seated around the table shook their heads, Mark nodded "All right. I'll see you all next month, same time, same place."

The rustle of paper, muted conversation and the scrape of chairs signaled the end of the meeting. David stood, gathered up his notes and made his way toward Steve.

"Thanks for the vote of confidence," he told him.

The sandy-haired minister flashed him a smile and spoke in a low voice. "Just don't blow it. Or we'll both be out on our ear."

A wry smile tugged at the corners of David's lips. "That makes me feel real secure."

The other man laughed and put his hand on David's arm. "Just kidding. I trust your instincts. But if you need a second opinion about any of your candidates, I'll be glad to talk to them, too."

"I may take you up on that."

"Will I see you at services Sunday?"

"Have I missed a week yet?"

"No. You're very faithful. I just wish I could have convinced you years ago to give religion a try."

"The timing wasn't right, I guess."

"Well, I'm glad you finally saw the light. Listen, call me some night next week and we'll go out for pizza. Monica will be in Chicago for a conference, and I'll be scavenging for food."

"You could learn to cook."

"My friend, I have been blessed with a number of talents. But cooking is not among them. My culinary forays have been a disaster. In fact, Monica has banned me from the stove and the oven when she's home. Trust me, she'll be glad if I eat out instead of messing up her kitchen. So call me, okay?"

A chuckle rumbled deep in David's chest. "You've got a deal."

"And don't worry about today's meeting. The board has always tended to err on the side of caution, but the members are working on that. Intellectually, they realize that nothing worth doing is accomplished without some risk, but it will take a little time for that understanding to reach their hearts. In the meantime, follow your instincts."

Another board member claimed Steve's attention, and David turned with a wave and headed toward the door. Despite Steve's parting words, he wondered if he was pushing too hard. Yet he prayed for guidance every day, and he was convinced God had led him to this place for a reason. He was also sure the Lord wouldn't want him to take the easy way out.

But the board's reaction was unsettling. If he made a wrong step, he could be ousted—just as his predecessor had been. And for a man who until recently had put a high priority on financial security, that was a scary thought. Growing up in a blue-collar family, where times had always been lean—and gotten even leaner when their father died too young and their mother had to take a job as a cook in a diner just to make ends meet—David had vowed to find a career that provided an income high enough to eliminate financial worries. He'd achieved that—in spades—in his former job. But over time he'd felt a call to do something else, something that made a difference in lives instead of balance sheets. Steve's call six months ago, alerting him to an upcoming opening at Uplink, had seemed almost providential. David had prayed about it—had even prayed that God not ask him to apply for it—but in the end, the call had been too strong to ignore. So he'd put his trust in God and taken a leap of faith. He just hoped he hadn't leapt into unemployment.

But as Steve had just reminded him, nothing worth doing was accomplished without some risk. And even if he failed, he would be able to take some comfort in knowing that he'd followed God's call and done his best.

David reached for the receiver, hesitated, then let his hand drop back to his desk. He wished he hadn't volunteered to contact Caroline about a story for the *Chronicle*. Seeing her once had been hard enough. Now he had to call and ask for her assistance. At least it was for a larger cause and not a personal favor. Still, it made him feel uneasy. And unsettled. In fact, he'd been feeling that way ever since his encounter with her the week before.

And he knew exactly why.

For one thing, their meeting had dredged up memories of the tragedy that had robbed his brother of his life. Had made him recall the day he'd been pulled out of a major negotiation session to take an urgent call that his usually efficient secretary hadn't seemed able to handle. He remembered muttering, "This better be important," as he swept past her with an irritated glance. He'd still been annoyed when he'd picked up the phone. Until he'd heard Caroline's almost hysterical voice on the other end of the crackling line, telling him between ragged sobs that Michael was dead.

David's gut had twisted into a hard knot, and he'd sagged against the desk, almost as if someone had delivered a physical blow to his midsection. He'd been too shocked to comprehend much else of what she'd said. And when she'd hung up, he'd sat there in stunned silence, until at last his secretary had knocked on the door to remind him that the high-powered group assembled in the next room was waiting for him.

It had been a nightmare day. And the two weeks that followed had been just as horrendous. He'd decided not to tell his mother, who was slipping away day by day, fearing that the news—if she even understood it— would strain her heart, which was already weak. So he'd stood alone at the funeral. Caroline had been beside him physically, but she'd been as unreachable as the distant peaks he'd spotted on his trek in the Himalayas last year. And looking at her devastated face, watching the way her hands shook, had only exacerbated his own pain—and guilt.

Seeing her again had brought all those memories back. So he shouldn't be surprised that the incident had unsettled him. Nor should he be surprised that the thought of contacting her again made him uneasy.

But he knew it was more than that. Knew that his feelings reflected something far deeper and less obvious, something he'd fiercely suppressed since the day Michael had escorted Caroline through the door of his mother's apartment and introduced her as his fiancée.

The fact was, from the first moment he'd laid eyes on her, David had been smitten. There was no other word for it. Nor any basis for it. He was an adult, after all. He'd been thirty-four when they met, not some teenager whose hormones could be whipped into a frenzy by the mere sight of a pretty face. In fact, he'd been so stunned by his unexpected reaction to her that he couldn't even recall much about that first meeting. He supposed he'd managed to sound coherent, because no one had acted as if he was behaving oddly. But he'd been so thrown that for the rest of Caroline and Michael's three-day visit, he had made it a point to avoid one-on-one conversations with her. He was afraid his tongue would get tangled up or, worse, that it would sabotage him and say something inappropriate. Such as, "I know you're engaged to my brother, but would you marry me, instead?"

That, of course, wasn't even a consideration. David

had never intruded on Michael's turf. Not as a child, not as a teenager, not as an adult. He loved his brother too much to do anything to jeopardize their relationship. In fact, if the truth was known, he'd always had a case of hero worship for him. He'd admired his sense of adventure, his willingness to take risks, his easygoing manner, his go-with-the-flow attitude. Not to mention his choice of women. Particularly his fiancée.

But if Caroline's beauty had bowled him over, he'd discovered other qualities about her in the next few days that had only added to her appeal. She'd been patient and kind with his failing mother, who had enjoyed some of her better days during their visit. He'd been struck by her lively intelligence, her generous spirit, her sense of justice and her passion for her work. In short, he'd been knocked off his feet.

In retrospect, David doubted that Caroline had even noticed him much during that visit. She'd had eyes only for Michael, and the soft light of love on her face when she looked at him had made David, for the first time in his life, jealous of his brother. It had also made him think about all the things he'd missed as he focused on launching his career to the exclusion of everything else—including love. Oh, he'd dated his share of women. But he'd never even considered a serious commitment. The trouble was, even though he'd opened the door to that possibility after her visit, he'd never met anyone who measured up to Caroline.

David knew that his impressions of her had been fleeting. Too fleeting to form the basis for any sort of rational attraction. Yet even as his brain reminded him of that, his heart refused to listen. For some reason, in that one brief visit, she'd touched him in a way no other woman had, before or since. She'd done so again, at Michael's funeral, though on that occasion the attraction was tempered by grief. And guilt. Even now, he could explain it no better than he had been able to two years before. He'd assumed that her appeal would dissipate over time, but he'd been wrong. The minute she'd stepped through the office door last week it had slammed against his chest with the same force that it had the first time they'd met.

As for how to handle his feelings—David had no idea. All he knew was that they were irrational, inappropriate and unsettling. Not to mention guilt-inducing. Caroline had loved Michael. She still did, if her reactions last week were any indication. And he couldn't intrude on his brother's turf. It hadn't felt right two and a half years ago, and it didn't feel right now. Even if the lady was willing or interested. And Caroline didn't fall into either of those categories. So his best plan was to make the call, ask for the favor and forget about her.

But considering the way his feelings had returned with such intensity after a two-year gap in contact, he suspected that plan was destined for failure.

"I have David Sloan on line three for you. Do you want to take the call?"

Caroline's hand jerked, making her pen squiggle across the copy she was editing. With dismay, she eyed the erratic red line sprawled across the typed page. So much for her usual neat, legible edits.

Why was David calling her? When he'd walked out the door last week, she'd been convinced that she'd never hear from him again. There had been a sense of finality about his visit, of closure. Now he was back. And she wasn't anxious to talk with him. It had taken her several days after his last visit to rebury the memories and pain it had dredged up. She didn't want to go through that again.

Still, she was curious. David didn't strike her as the kind of man who did things without a great deal of thought. Nor without good reason. Whatever the purpose of his call, she assumed it was important.

Shifting the phone on her ear, she laid down her pen and rotated her chair so that her back was toward the newsroom. "Go ahead and put it through, Mary. Thanks."

A second later, David's voice came over the line. "Caroline?"

"Yes, hi. I didn't expect to hear from you again so soon."

"I didn't expect to be calling. But we had a discussion earlier this week at the Uplink board meeting about the need for publicity, and I offered to contact you to see if the *Chronicle* might be interested in running a piece about the organization."

So this was a business call. She hadn't expected that, either. But it was much easier to deal with. The knot of tension in her stomach eased.

In journalist mode, she swiveled her chair back toward her desk, reached for a pen and drew a pad of paper toward her. "We're always looking for good story leads. But I have to confess that I'm not familiar with Uplink."

"That's the problem. Not enough people are. And that hampers our ability to fully realize our mission."

"Which is?"

"We target gifted high school juniors in difficult environments and match them with mentors in participating businesses for summer internships to provide them with a taste of a real-world work environment. We hope the experience gives them not only a stimulating summer job, but an incentive to continue with their education. Then we follow up with ongoing support groups to ensure that we don't lose them after their internships."

"You mentioned some of this last week. Sounds worthwhile."

"We think so. But the organization is only three years old—still a fledgling. There's a lot more we could do if this really takes off. For that to happen, though, we need to heighten awareness."

"What sort of article did you have in mind?"

"I'm not sure. One of the board members, Rachel Harris, handles publicity and communication. She can follow up with more information if you're interested in pursuing this. My role was just to get a foot in the door."

"All right." Caroline jotted the woman's name down, then laid the pen aside. "Have her give me a call. If we can find a good angle, it might make an interesting article."

"That would be great. We'd appreciate it."

"Like I said, we're always looking for good stories. But I have to admit I'm curious about how you became connected with the group. This seems far removed from your previous job."

The momentary silence on the other end of the line told her he was surprised by the question. And so was she. She hadn't planned to introduce anything personal to their conversation. The comment had just popped out.

Despite his initial reaction, however, David's tone was conversational when he responded. "It is. I'd been doing a lot of soul-searching for the past few years, and I began to feel a need to do something with my life that had more purpose than just making a lot of money."

A melancholy smile whispered at the corners of her mouth. "Michael used to say almost exactly the same thing."

Her comment startled him. No one had ever compared him to his brother before. It made him feel good, and odd at the same time. "I guess that's true," he acknowledged. "But my impetus was different. It grew out of long conversations with God."

"You're right. Michael was driven by a deep sense of ethics versus faith, and by a desire to help improve the human race."

"I guess our goal was the same, then. Just not the motivation."

"Well…I wish you luck with the job. It sounds like good work. I'll be expecting Rachel's call."

"Great. We appreciate anything you can do. Take care."

The line went dead, and Caroline put the phone back in its holder. She still wasn't sure why she'd asked about his new job. It had moved them out of a safe topic and into touchy personal territory. Maybe it had just been her professional curiosity kicking in. Since asking questions was part of her job, it made sense that she would delve a little deeper with David. Didn't it?

The answer came to her in a flash. No. If she'd wanted to avoid personal discussion, if she'd wanted to get off the phone as fast as possible, she'd have ended the conversation instead of detouring to a more personal line of questioning.

Okay, so much for her first theory. She tried another one on for size. Maybe contact with David made her feel, in some way, connected with Michael. As if, through David, Michael was still somehow part of her life in a tangible way. She and David were the only ones who had really known, and loved, the man she'd planned to marry. Her mother was a great sounding board, and she'd listened with infinite patience when Caroline had reached the stage of grief where she could talk about her fiancé, and share some of her memories. But her mother had no firsthand knowledge of him beyond that brief Christmas visit to both families.

David, on the other hand, had years' worth of memories of Michael. Ones that Caroline didn't have. His bond to the prize-winning photojournalist was as strong as hers, in a different way. Maybe, on some subconscious level, she wanted to tap into them. To supplement her own memories of the man she'd loved, who had talked of his past only on rare occasions. And maybe she also wanted to shore up her memories. In recent months it had grown harder for her to picture Michael's face without the aid of a photograph. She'd already begun to forget the unique sound of his voice. Along with the feel of his touch. She didn't want to let go of Michael, but he was slipping away, bit by bit. And that frightened her. Perhaps her reaching out to David today had been driven by fear, and by a desire to connect with the one man who had the best chance of keeping Michael alive for her.

Yes, no doubt that was it.

Satisfied, Caroline reached for her red pen and pulled the copy back toward her. Only then did she realize that her jerky squiggle bore a striking resemblance to half of a heart. How appropriate, she reflected with a pang. Half a heart was exactly what she felt like she had. The rest had died along with the man she loved.

And there was nothing David Sloan could do to fix that.

"Here's some information on Uplink. And I asked Mitch about it, too." Tess Jackson laid the material on Caroline's desk, taking the seat the managing editor waved her into.

"Did he know anything?"

"Not a lot. It's targeted more toward inner-city schools. But he made a few calls, and in general heard glowing reports from his colleagues. He thought it would be a very worthwhile feature. I do, too, from a journalistic perspective."

After a quick scan of the material, Caroline leaned back in her chair and steepled her fingers. She respected Mitch Jackson, a former cop whose innovative work as a hands-on high school principal had drawn state-wide notice. His personal interventions had steered dozens of wayward students back to the right path. She also respected his wife's assessment of the story potential.

That was why Tess had been promoted in two short years to assistant editor.

"Okay. What kind of angle do you propose?"

"Human interest. I think we should include some history of Uplink, but focus on a couple of the students who've been through the program and talk about what a difference it made in their lives. We'd want to include interviews with the businesses that were involved, the students and the executive director, as well as the chairman of the board."

"Sounds good. Who should we assign?"

"As a matter of fact, I'd like to take this one. I think I have a good feel for the subject, given Mitch's work at the high school. Unless you want to do it. After that story you did on gangs last year, you've got an understanding of the problems out there, and the need for intervention. Besides, it should be a meaty piece, and you like to tackle those."

Caroline had already thought this through. And had come to the conclusion that whatever her motives in yesterday's conversation with David, it wasn't wise to prolong contact with him. In addition to the painful memories that were rekindled, there were too many unresolved questions that she didn't want to dredge up. Like, why had David insisted on putting his mother in an extended-care facility so soon after their visit, breaking a promise both brothers had made to her years before? She'd overheard the two men discussing it one evening, in subdued tones near the Christmas tree, and while she hadn't been able to make out the words—nor had she tried to—the frustration in both voices had been unmistakable.

In the end, she'd sided with Michael. Martha Sloan might have been a bit vague, but Caroline hadn't seen any evidence of advanced Alzheimer's during their visit. Certainly not enough to warrant institutionalization. David had agreed to hold off, but then had called Michael a month later to tell him that he was going to move her into a nursing facility anyway. Michael had asked him to wait until they could discuss it in person, when he and Caroline returned later in the year for their wedding, but David had refused. The brothers hadn't talked again until the night before Michael died, when David had called to tell him that their mother had suffered a mild heart attack.

It was odd, really. Back then, David hadn't struck her as uncaring or cavalier. Or as a man who broke his promises. He still didn't. She found it hard to think of him as someone who would disregard the wishes of a person he loved. Yet the facts all pointed to that. And it wasn't something she respected. Nor wanted to discuss. But if they continued to have contact, it would no doubt come up, since it had been such a point of contention between the brothers. As a result, it was best if she let someone else handle the story.

"No. You do it, Tess. I'll refer Rachel Harris to you when she calls."

"You're sure?"

"Absolutely."

"Okay. I'll dive in as soon as we hear from Rachel. Any special timing on this?"

From what David had said, the group wanted to raise its profile as soon as possible. Of course, that couldn't be a factor in her decision. She had to do what was best for the paper and for the readers. Still, there was a piece about home schooling scheduled for two editions down the road that was pretty timeless. She checked the run list.

"If we bump the home-school piece a week, we could use this March twenty-seventh. Do you think you can have it ready by then?"

"Assuming the Uplink people get back to us right away, that shouldn't be a problem," Tess assured her.

"Okay. Let's shoot for that. But that deadline isn't written in stone. We can shift it later if necessary."

"Got it. Anything else?"

"No. That should do it. Let me know if you run into any snags." Caroline turned back toward her computer.

"Will do. How's the budget coming?"

Grimacing, Caroline shook her head, her focus still on the screen in front of her. "I didn't go into journalism to crunch numbers," she grumbled.

"Somebody has to do it. And better you than me."

With a mirthless grin, Caroline waved her out. "Thanks for the sympathy."

"At least the budget will distract you from the nasty letters we've been getting about that story we ran on the group home for juvenile offenders," Tess offered as she exited.

"Good point." Though the article had been straightforward and objective, neighbors of the home had chosen to view it as an endorsement. They hadn't appreciated that, and had been very vocal in their disapproval of the paper's perceived position.

If the budget work distracted her from that can of

worms, maybe there was a plus to it, Caroline conceded. And she'd be even more grateful if it distracted her from David. She didn't want to think about him anymore. Despite his calm, in-control demeanor, his presence in her life had been disruptive. For reasons that eluded her, she couldn't seem to quash thoughts of him. Maybe crunching numbers would do the trick. That would require her absolute and total concentration.

And for some reason, she had a feeling it would take something that attention-demanding to keep thoughts of David at bay.

Chapter Three

As he was being introduced, David surveyed the students in the high school auditorium from his seat on the stage. Most looked bored and made no pretense of listening to Principal Charles Elliot's comments. Others were scribbling in notebooks or staring into space. Out of the hundred or hundred-and-fifty juniors, David estimated that maybe ten percent were interested. It was about the same percentage he'd run into in many of the inner-city schools. But if this presentation went as well as previous ones, he expected that percentage would double or even triple. He couldn't ask for more than that. Besides, they only had places for twenty-five students in the program this summer, anyway.

When the principal turned to him, David sent an encouraging glance to the two former Uplink students seated beside him, then rose and moved forward. He shook the man's hand, pulled the microphone from its stand and came out from behind the podium. His stance was casual, his tone conversational, his attitude approachable.

"Good afternoon. As Mr. Elliot said, I'm David Sloan, the executive director of Uplink. With me today are two students who've participated in our program. For the next forty-five minutes, we'd like to talk with you about an opportunity that could change your life forever."

With passion, conviction and enthusiasm, David explained the principles behind Uplink and spoke of the successes already documented by the program. The testimonials from the two students, who were now attending college on scholarships, were also powerful, making it clear that for committed students, Uplink opened doors to a future that would otherwise have been inaccessible. Neither they nor David made it sound easy, because it wasn't. It took talent and dedication to get in, and the rigorous screening and ongoing evaluation process intimidated a lot of kids. Participation required guts and focus and lots of hard work. But for those who persevered, the rewards were great.

By the time they finished, David figured that a good twenty-five percent of the students in the audience had been captivated enough to at least pay attention. Not bad. If five or six ended up applying, he'd consider it a good day's work.

They stayed around after the presentation ended in case any of the students wanted to speak with them one-on-one, but it didn't surprise David when only a couple came forward. In North St. Louis, where drugs and gangs were rampant and academics wasn't always valued or supported at home, few students would publicly acknowledge an interest in a program like Uplink. Those who decided to apply would follow up without fanfare, in confidence. David understood that and didn't push. That first step took courage, and he considered it a good barometer of genuine interest.

As he thanked the two students who had accompanied him, David turned to find Charles Elliot approaching. The man took David's hand in a firm grip.

"I appreciate your coming today. I expect you'll hear from a few of the students."

"I hope so. I understand that we've had a couple of students from here in the program every year since its inception."

"That's right. I'm a great believer in Uplink, and I talk it up whenever I get the chance. Can I walk you out?"

"Thanks."

David reached for his leather jacket, which he'd slung over the back of his folding chair, and slid his arms into the sleeves as they headed toward the exit. The assembly had marked the end of the school day for the juniors, and they'd cleared out with a speed that rivaled a race car in the home stretch. The rest of the students had been dismissed ten or fifteen minutes earlier. The two men's footsteps echoed hollowly as they walked down the long, deserted corridor toward the exit.

A classroom door opened as they passed, and a woman in a paint-spattered smock, her short black hair a mass of tight curls, spoke when she caught sight of them.

"Oh, Charles…I'm glad I caught you. Do you have a second to sign that exhibit application?"

"Of course." He turned back to David in apology.

"I'll be right with you. Sylvia is the art teacher, and she's trying to get some of our students' work included in a traveling exhibition sponsored by a national company."

"Take your time. I'm in no hurry."

While he waited, David examined some of the artwork that hung in the hallway near the classroom door. A variety of mediums was represented, and many of the pieces were impressive. He stopped to examine a striking abstract watercolor, then moved on to a pen-and-ink sketch of a mother and child, caught by their poignant expressions of disillusionment. But it was the next series of three black-and-white photographs that mesmerized him.

The first was a portrait of an older woman wearing wire-rimmed glasses, her close-cropped black hair peppered with gray. She sat in front of a window, a bit off center, at a chipped, Formica table, one side of her face in sharp relief, the other shadowed. One work-worn hand rested on the Bible in her lap, the other lay beside a daffodil on the scratched surface of the table. Behind her, the paint on the walls was chipped, the windowsill scarred. Part of a calendar was visible, and the photograph of the month featured a quiet, peaceful country lane bordered by apple trees laden with blossoms. The photographer had titled the photo "Beauty."

The next photo was just as powerful. Two small children in mismatched clothes sat on a concrete stoop. The low angle of the shot drew the eye upward, past the broken windows of a dingy tenement to the open expanse of sky above. The children's raised faces were illuminated with an almost transcendent light as they gazed at the clouds drifting overhead. It bore the title "Imagine."

The last picture also displayed a masterful use of light and a stellar aptitude for composition. There were no people visible in the shot. Just the shadow of a man, his hand extended toward another smaller shadow that was reaching up to him. The dark outlines stretched across a good part of the frame, covering the broken bottles and garbage that littered the foreground. They were poised at the base of a flight of steps that led upward and out of the frame to a higher, unknown and unseen place. The camera had caught them as they prepared to ascend. It was titled "Together."

Though the images were stark and bleak at first glance, that wasn't what caught David's interest. While the subjects were different, they shared a powerful common theme—hope. Captured in a simple, but dramatic and symbolic style. David was overwhelmed.

Until Michael had discovered his talent for photography, David had never paid much attention to that art beyond the occasional fuzzy family snapshots his mother sometimes took. But as Michael pursued his passion, as he learned to work magic with a couple of lenses and the striking use of angle and light, David had learned to appreciate the potential and power of a camera in the hands of a master. Like the photographer of these images, Michael had had the ability to touch hearts, to communicate messages that continued to resonate long after people put the photo aside. It was a great gift, one that had allowed Michael to find his true calling. And the photographer of these photos seemed to share that gift.

"They're pretty amazing, aren't they?"

Charles had rejoined him, and David turned to the principal. "Amazing is an apt description. Were these done by a student?"

"Yes. Jared Poole. They were part of an art assignment for Sylvia's junior class."

Looking back at the photos, David shook his head. "I hope he plans to pursue his talent."

When the other man didn't respond, David turned toward him again. Charles's face was troubled, and he gave a resigned sigh before he spoke. "Jared has some…problems. He got involved with a gang a couple of years ago, and he's had some minor run-ins with the law. Nothing too serious—yet. But he's headed in the wrong direction. Truancy has also been an issue. He has a lot to offer, including very strong writing skills, but he just doesn't make school a priority."

"That's too bad. What's the family situation like?" Since taking the job at Uplink, David had already learned that without support at home, there was little chance that problem students would buckle down at school.

"Not good. He lives with his grandmother. That's her picture, in fact." He indicated the photo of the woman with the Bible. "His father disappeared before he was born. His mother died of a drug overdose when Jared was about eight. It's just been him and his grandmother ever since. I've met her, and I know she loves him very much. But she works nights, cleaning offices, so Jared is on his own a lot. The gang became a surrogate family for him. I've tried to talk to him, but I don't think I've gotten through. I did hear through the grapevine that he's trying to break his gang ties. But even if that's true, it's not easy to do."

In his brief tenure at Uplink, David had heard any number of similar stories. They always left him feeling helpless, wishing he could do more. But he knew his limitations. He couldn't take a personal interest in every troubled teenager he ran across. The best he could do was pour his heart and soul into Uplink and hope that his efforts would make a difference in at least a few lives.

Charles led the way toward the front door, sending David off with a firm handshake and another thank-you.

"Let me know if any of our students contact you. I'll be glad to give you my thoughts on whether they'd make good candidates for Uplink," he offered.

"I'll do that."

As David stepped outside, a gust of bitter March wind assaulted him, and he turned up his collar and stuck his hands in the pockets of his jacket. Late-afternoon shadows from the chainlink fence around the school slanted across the buckled sidewalk, and dilapidated buildings, crumbling concrete and rusty metal were all he could see in any direction. The place reeked of decay and despair.

But inside the building behind him, captured in those stark black-and-white photos, hope lived amidst the gloom and desperation around him. And as he walked to his car, he prayed that the young man who had captured it in those images would also find a way to incorporate it into his life.

* * *

A knock sounded on her office door, and Caroline looked up. "Come in, Tess. What's up?"

"Sorry to interrupt, but Bruce was injured at school. Some scenery he was painting for the school play fell, and he needs a few stitches. Mitch is taking him to the hospital, and I'd like to meet them there."

"Of course. You don't need to ask permission. Just go."

"The thing is, I was supposed to attend a presentation today by David Sloan at one of the high schools, and then interview him afterward at his office. That was the last interview I needed for the story. If I have to reschedule, I'll miss the deadline."

A few seconds of silence ticked by while Caroline considered her options. She could offer to do the interview and pass her notes on to Tess. They'd worked together doing research and interviews on a number of complex stories. But that meant she'd have to deal with David again. Or she could just reschedule the story. The home-schooling piece was finished and could be dropped into the Uplink slot with no problem. That would delay the Uplink story by a week, but they'd made no promises about when it would appear.

"Let's reschedule," Caroline decided.

"Okay. I'll give him a call."

The matter decided, Caroline went back to editing the next week's edition—only to be interrupted again a few minutes later by Tess.

"Sorry to cause problems, Caroline. But David Sloan says he only has one more presentation, and it's not for two weeks. If we put this off, we'll have to push the story into mid-April."

Not good. Caroline had only the home-schooling piece in reserve. If she used it for the next issue, they'd need the Uplink story for the following edition. Or else she'd have to scramble to come up with another meaty feature. All at once her options shrank.

"Okay. I'll cover for you today."

"Are you sure? I guess I could just let Mitch handle things at the hospital."

Caroline heard the uncertainty in Tess's voice and recalled the difficult time her assistant editor had had with her son just three years before, when she'd moved to St. Louis after losing her job due to downsizing at a small-town Missouri newspaper. She'd found a new life in St. Louis—and a new love in Mitch Jackson, who had helped her get her son back on the right path when he'd fallen in with the wrong group. Caroline understood Tess's need to be present today.

"Go ahead. Don't worry about it. Just give me the details and I'll handle this. Emergencies happen."

Gratitude filled the other woman's eyes. "Have I told you lately that you're a great boss?"

A flush crept up Caroline's neck. "Hey, work is important but family comes first. Let David know I'll be taking your place. Then get out of here."

As she watched Tess make a hasty exit, Caroline thought about what she'd just said. She hadn't always been as understanding about personal obligations. There had been a time when she'd put the highest priority on her work, on rising through the ranks of journalism to nab a top spot. A time when she'd looked with disdain on those who put their personal life ahead of getting the story. Then she'd met Michael. Committed to his work, passionate about truth, he'd nevertheless had perspective, recognizing the critical importance of balance. He'd worked hard, but he'd also made time for other things—and for people.

In retrospect, Caroline had often wondered if he'd known at some unconscious level that his stay on earth would be brief. It was as if he had been driven to savor each second, to suck every drop of sweetness from each moment, to treat each new day as a gift, as an opportunity to learn and to grow and to become a better person. That attitude had carried over to his work, compelling him to portray even the most horrible circumstances with empathy and compassion. Even images that had made her cringe in their rawness had been infused with humanity. And in his portraits, he always captured the essence of those he photographed, putting a face on tragedy in a way that touched people and softened even the most cynical hearts. That had been his gift.

With Michael, Caroline had learned to see with new eyes. And to forge a new perspective, one that recognized the importance of love and relationships. It was a lesson she never wanted to forget. And the situation with Tess was just one way she'd been able to put that philosophy into action.

Unfortunately, it also put her in the line of fire. She didn't relish another encounter with David. But she was a professional. She'd treat this just like any other interview. And when she was finished, there'd be no reason for their paths to cross again. Tess would write the article, the *Chronicle* would run it and Uplink would have the publicity it had sought.

End of story.

As the principal did the introductions, David scanned the crowd. He'd gotten Tess's message just as he walked out the door of his office, so he knew Caroline would be in the audience instead of the assistant editor. And he had mixed feelings about that.

Even though his primary purpose in going to the *Chronicle* had been to give her the medallion and to apologize, he'd also hoped to discover that her captivating charm had lessened. Instead, he'd found that the opposite was true. And he still had no logical explanation for it. All he knew was that his safest course was to steer clear of her in the future. That's why he hadn't been all that keen on contacting her about the Uplink story. But at least that had been by phone. He hadn't had to look into those appealing hazel eyes. And he'd figured that would be the end of it.

Now she was in the audience. Afterward, she'd come back to his office to do an interview. And despite all of the rational reasons why her presence was bad, he couldn't stop the sudden rush of happiness and anticipation that swept through his heart, like an unexpected, glorious burst of sun streaming through the clouds on a gray, overcast day.

She wasn't hard to pick out. Her hair would give her away in any crowd, but especially here, where the glints of copper shimmered in the bright overhead light, and her fair complexion stood out in the sea of ebony faces. He watched as she withdrew a notebook from her large shoulder bag and flipped it open, then settled back in her seat in the last row and looked toward the stage. When their gazes connected, he gave her a welcoming smile. Her lips turned up just the slightest bit in response before she shifted her attention to the principal, who was just about to introduce David. And he better get focused, too, David reminded himself. He needed to concentrate on the presentation and forget about Caroline for the next forty-five minutes.

It wasn't easy to switch gears, but once he started talking, his focus became absolute, as it always did. No matter how often he gave this talk, his enthusiasm for the program and his passion for the principles it represented came through loud and clear.

None of which was lost on Caroline. Though she'd had only a few minutes to prep, she'd given the material Tess had collected and her assistant editor's notes from previous interviews a cursory review. She'd been impressed by Uplink and what it had accomplished in a short time, and she was just as impressed by David's sincerity and obvious commitment to the program. His presentation was dynamic and engaging, and she noticed as he spoke that a number of students who had at first seemed disinterested began to pay closer attention.

By the time he and the Uplink students he'd brought along had finished, the boredom and cynicism in the audience had shifted toward respect and interest. She'd learned enough about the North St. Louis high school environment while working on her gang series to know that David's accomplishment was no small feat. Outsiders were typically viewed with suspicion. And Caucasian outsiders were often viewed with hostility. But there had been an appreciable change in the mood in the auditorium. Caroline was impressed.

As the presentation wound down and the students were dismissed, Caroline gathered up her things, rose and slipped on her coat. She waited by the back door as David said a few words to the two Uplink students, shook hands with the principal then made his way toward her.

"Thanks for coming on such short notice," he said as he drew close.

"It wasn't a problem. Tess and I have worked together on other stories."

"She said her son had been injured?"

"I don't think it's anything serious. It sounded like he might need a few stitches. But she had some problems with him a few years ago, and now she tries extra hard to be there for him."

"That's commendable. I wish more parents felt that way. Especially parents of students like these."

"I know. I did a series a year or so ago on gang culture, about the power gangs exert over their members and how gangs become a surrogate family in the absence of a real one. The problem of uninvolved parents is very real. And not just in this part of town."

"It makes you wonder why some people have kids, if they aren't willing to take on the responsibilities of parenthood."

"Mitch Jackson, Tess's husband, could give you an earful on that subject. He's the principal at one of the high schools in a pretty affluent area of the city. His stories about uninvolved parents are unbelievable."

David shook his head. "Throw in a cycle of poverty and a culture that doesn't value education, and the problem is only exacerbated. It's an uphill battle, that's for sure. But at least Uplink is trying to offer a few kids a way out." The somber expression on his face gave way to a grin. "But I'm done lecturing for today. Are you ready to leave?"

"Yes."

As they exited the auditorium and walked down the hall toward the front door, Caroline reached into her bag for her keys.

"Where are you parked?" David asked.

"Just down the street."

"I'll walk you to your car."

"You don't need to do that."

"Yes, I do. This isn't the best area of town."

As they stepped through the door, Caroline gave him a wry glance. "I've been in worse places."

True, David mused, recalling Caroline's quick summary of her career when he'd inquired, shortly after they met. Two years on the crime beat for a paper in Atlanta, three years in Washington, D.C., covering politics, then domestic and European assignments for AP before being stationed in a hot zone in the Middle East. How had Michael managed to live with the knowledge that the woman he loved was putting herself in danger day in and day out?

As he looked down at her face, lifted to his, the afternoon sunlight infused her skin with warmth and highlighted a small scar on her right temple, near her hairline. Without stopping to think, he raised his finger and traced the thin white line with a gentle touch. "Is this a souvenir of one of those places?"

The husky quality of his voice, his tender touch, the deep caring in his warm brown eyes so surprised Caroline that for a second she could only stare at him.

At her stunned reaction, David let his hand drop back to his side. Talk about a dumb move. The last thing he needed to do was tip his hand about the embarrassing—and guilt-inducing—feelings he'd been trying to deal with for two and a half years. Besides, they were all one-sided. Caroline had been head-over-heels in love with Michael. She still was, if her reaction to the medallion had been any indication. David had never even been on her radar, except in a negative way after Michael's death. And he wanted to keep it that way. It was much safer.

Shoving his hand in his pocket, he forced his lips into a smile. "Sorry. That's none of my business." He started down the sidewalk, and Caroline fell into step beside him.

"I didn't mind the question." It had just been the way it was asked that had startled her. "And the answer is no. This is of a more recent vintage."

She didn't offer more, and although he was curious, he didn't press her. He needed to stay away from personal topics. "Do you have directions to my office?"

"Yes. It's in Maplewood, right?" Caroline was familiar with the close-in suburb.

"Mmm-hmm. How about we meet there in fifteen minutes?"

"Sounds good."

By the time Caroline pulled up in front of the modest, storefront office for Uplink, she was still mulling over the few seconds at the school when David had touched her—and the disturbing look in his eyes. Though he'd masked it quickly, she'd had a brief glimpse of something she was tempted to call attraction. But she had to be wrong. They'd only met a few times. Even the Christmas she'd visited with Michael, she and David hadn't spoken at any length. She'd spent more time with their mother, figuring the two brothers might want some time alone. And she'd thought little about him since. She hardly knew him. Yet he'd looked at her in a way that made her feel he knew her. And that he'd thought about her a great deal.

Still, she could be jumping to conclusions. David seemed to be a caring man. His involvement with Uplink was proof of that. Maybe he looked at everyone in that same kind, concerned manner. Yet that didn't make sense, either, not after the way he'd treated his mother, breaking a promise both brothers had made to her and disregarding Michael's wishes. In any case, she figured she was reading far too much into a three-second interlude.

Putting thoughts of the incident aside, Caroline slung her bag over her shoulder, stepped out of her car and walked down the busy street toward David's office. Maplewood was enjoying an incredible resurgence, and she made a mental note to do some brainstorming at the next *Chronicle* staff meeting to see if they could come up with a story to highlight the transformation.

When she stepped through the door, a solid, big-boned, middle-aged woman smiled at her from behind a reception desk. "You must be Caroline. Come right in, honey. David had to take a call, but he'll be with you in a minute. Can I get you some coffee?" Her husky voice had a pleasing, rough-around-the-edges quality.

"Yes, thanks. That would be great."

"Cream or sugar?"

"Black is fine. But I can get it." Caroline took note of the coffeemaker off to one side as she dropped her shoulder bag on a chair.

Ignoring her, the woman came out from behind the desk and headed toward the small cabinet. "You just sit. Take the load off. Not that you have much load to take off." A chuckle rumbled deep in the woman's chest as she filled the cup. Then she turned back toward Caroline with a smile that showcased the dazzling white teeth in her dusky face. "Here you go, honey. Nothing like a good cup of coffee late in the afternoon to give you a second wind. I'm Ella, by the way. After Ella Fitzgerald. My mother was a great fan of hers. Hoped I'd be blessed with a voice like she had, too. No such luck, though. I could never carry a tune in a bucket."

With a smile, Caroline took her proffered hand. "It's nice to meet you, Ella."

"I'll let David know you're here."

"Thanks."

While Caroline waited, she surveyed the small reception room. Though the surroundings were pleasant and clean, they were pretty bare-bones. Ella's desk was an older-style metal unit, and the wall behind her was lined with two utilitarian file cabinets. The small grouping of furniture in the waiting room was an eclectic mix of pieces that made Caroline wonder if they might be donations from a variety of sources. There were a few homey touches, though, including a plaque that said, "Bloom where you are planted," and some photos of students receiving awards, plus a table next to the window laden with a variety of flourishing plants.

"Someone has a green thumb," Caroline commented when Ella returned. "Or should I say green hand?"

"David says that I'm turning the office into a greenhouse," Ella told her with another chuckle. "But I like to watch things grow. Plants—or people. Those were all half-dead castoffs when I inherited them. But they just needed a little attention. TLC goes a long way."

Before Caroline could respond, the door behind Ella opened and David motioned her in. "Sorry for the delay. I see Ella took care of you." He nodded to the coffee cup in her hands.

"Yes. It was just what I needed."

"She has a knack for that." David sent the receptionist an affectionate look.

"Now that one's a flatterer," Ella warned Caroline, though it was clear she was pleased by David's compliment. "And I could tell you some other things about him, too."

"Uh-oh. I don't like the sound of that. Come on in, Caroline, before Ella says something I'll live to regret."

Caroline smiled and moved past David into his

office. As she took a seat at the small table he indicated in the corner, she again noted the bare-bones nature of the Uplink offices. David's U-shaped desk module and the conference table were wood-grained Formica, while the filing cabinets were gray metal. It was obvious that very little of the money intended for the Uplink program was funneled to administrative expenses. A few personal touches warmed up the room, including some family photos that she surveyed with interest, and an exotic-looking woven wall hanging.

The contrast between David's present work environment and the plush offices he must have enjoyed in his old job struck Caroline. Michael had said he brokered multimillion-dollar mergers and acquisitions, rubbing elbows with the movers and shakers in business. What had made him give all that up?

"I'm new at this interviewing game. What can I tell you about Uplink that Tess hasn't already covered?" David asked, interrupting her musings.

Uplink. That's why she was here, Caroline reminded herself, refocusing her attention. From Tess's notes, she knew the other woman had most of the background information she needed. And Caroline had jotted down a great deal of information during the presentation that could be used to flesh out the story. A few quotes from the executive director would round out the article.

"I don't need much," she told him. "Tess has done a thorough job already. And the meeting today was very helpful. Just tell me a little bit about your role."

David complied, explaining the fundraising, recruiting and administrative duties of the job. But he focused on the recruiting aspect, which he considered to be vital.

"We want to attract the students who can benefit the most from our program," he explained. "For the first few years, my predecessor devoted his time to getting the program established. Now that it is, we're taking a more aggressive approach to recruiting, doing outreach and presentations in schools where there is a high incidence of students who drop out, or where truancy is a problem. The mission of the organization is to reach out to those most in need of intervention, and since I took over on the first of the year, we've moved more and more in that direction."

"Tell me a little about your background, David. This seems like quite a switch from your previous job."

"It's night and day," he acknowledged, then proceeded to confirm what Michael had told her about his high-stakes business career.

"What prompted you to make such a radical change?"

"A friend of mine is on the Uplink board. He told me several months ago that the position would be opening up, and asked if I'd be interested. I don't think he expected me to say yes, but I surprised him. And myself, I might add. I'd been doing a lot of soul-searching about where I wanted to be five years down the road, and I'd come to the conclusion that I needed more to show for my life than a list of mergers and acquisitions I'd helped broker. I wanted to be able to say that my life stood for something more lasting, more important, than dollars and deals. I took to heart something Mother Teresa once said—'God has not called me to be successful, God has called me to be faithful.' And after a lot of prayer and discernment, God led me here."

"This isn't a faith-based organization, though, is it?"

"No. But helping young people get their lives together is one way of doing God's work."

Caroline was again struck by the quiet, deep faith that seemed to guide David's life. Since she hadn't had a chance to probe about it when they'd met, she took advantage of the opportunity. Closing her notebook, she laid it aside. "Can I ask you a question, off the record?"

A flicker of surprise—followed by caution—registered on his face. "Sure."

"Michael told me once that you weren't raised in a home where faith was discussed very much. And his faith was marginal, at best. How did you find your way to God?"

A smile touched the corners of David's mouth. "To be honest, I didn't. He found me."

Curious, Caroline studied him. "If this gets too personal, just tell me to back off, but I'd be interested to hear more about that."

"May I ask why?"

It was a fair question. If she was making personal queries, he had a right to do the same. "I guess I'm intrigued by faith. Maybe even drawn to it. I was raised in a household where faith was important, but over time I just drifted away. When we met that Christmas, there was something about the way you talked about your faith that caught my attention. I'd have liked to talk more to you about it then, but there just wasn't time. Then Michael died, and I didn't think about God for a long time. But in the past few months my interest has started to grow again. To be honest, I'm not sure why."

"I don't think that's an uncommon experience. My initial forays were pretty tentative, too, and I didn't understand the reason. I just felt the need to connect with something bigger, some higher power. And when I did, three or four years ago, my life started to change. Not always in ways that were comfortable, though. This job is a good example. I'm sure Michael told you that we grew up in a lower-income, blue-collar family. Money was always tight. Too tight. I decided that when I grew up I would find a career that gave me financial security. But once I had that, I realized it wasn't enough. That's when I started to listen to the Lord's voice. To put my trust in Him, and to follow the path He was leading me to."

"So one day you just woke up and decided to give up the life you'd created and take this job?"

"It wasn't quite that simple." He leaned back in his chair, and his face grew thoughtful. "I struggled with it for a long time. But my options were limited before Mom died."

Caroline wanted to ask why, but he continued before she had a chance to voice the question.

"After she was gone, I talked to my friend on the Uplink board, who's a minister. I also forced myself to get out of my rut, out of my usual environment, away from the familiar, hoping that a change of scene would give me some new insights. One year, I took a trip down the Amazon. The next, a trek in the Himalayas. That's a souvenir from the second trip." He indicated the woven wall-hanging Caroline had noticed earlier.

Taken aback, Caroline stared at him, trying to reconcile this David with the picture Michael had painted of his cautious, introverted brother, whose idea of an "adventure" vacation—according to Michael—was spending four days camping on the shores of Lake Michigan.

He flashed her a brief grin. "I surprised myself, too. As Michael obviously told you, risk-taking isn't in my nature, and those trips were a stretch for me. But they did help me think about things in a different way. Get a new outlook. Other than those adventures, though, I've led a pretty boring life."

Caroline's eyes grew flat, like landscape thrown in shadow by a dark cloud. "Boring isn't so bad."

Her sudden bleak expression didn't get past David, and he recalled her comment at the *Chronicle,* that she'd seen enough blood, sweat and tears to last a lifetime. "It can be if it traps you in a life that keeps you from growing in your faith or as a person."

"Maybe." She didn't sound convinced.

"Anyway, after a lot of thought, a lot of prayer and a lot of conversations with my friend, I found my way back to God. And that's how I ended up here."

"Any regrets?"

"Not a one. At least not about the job, and about turning my life over to God." Then his face grew pensive. "But there are other things I would do differently if I had a second chance."

Caroline wondered if he was thinking about his decision to institutionalize his mother. Or about his estrangement from Michael. But she'd asked enough questions today. If she delved any deeper, he could very well turn the tables on her and ask about her regrets. And that wasn't something she wanted to discuss.

Reaching for her tote, Caroline stuffed her notebook inside and slung it over her shoulder, then rose. "Well, thank you for your time today. We're planning to run the article in next week's edition."

Standing, David reached over to grip her hand with his strong, firm fingers. "Thanks for the coverage."

"Like I said when you called, we're always looking for a good story."

When he continued to hold her hand, she searched his eyes. They were a soft, quiet brown, as still and deep as a spring tucked into the shadowed crevices of a woodland grotto. She had the oddest impression that he was looking right into her heart, touching her pain, seeing the secrets and doubts she'd kept long buried.

Feeling off balance, she pulled her hand free and turned to go. "We'll send you some extra copies."

"I'd appreciate that."

He opened his office door, and when she stepped through Ella gave her a smile.

"Well, that didn't take long. Did you get everything you need, honey?"

"Yes. Thanks."

"I figured David would take care of you."

As Caroline exited the office and made her way back to her car, the receptionist's words echoed in her mind. She knew the woman's comment had been in reference to the story. But for some reason, Caroline sensed that it was true on a deeper level. That if she gave him the chance, David would take care of her in far more personal ways as well.

She had no idea where that absurd intuition had come from. She and David had nothing in common beyond a link to Michael. They didn't even know each other very well. She must be losing it.

There was a time when Caroline had relied on her instincts, when she'd trusted them. But if today's experience was any indication, she'd better be a little more cautious about putting her faith in them in the future.

Because this one had been way off base.

Chapter Four

J ared Poole.

The name stared back at David from the Uplink application. So his presentation had reached the gifted photographer. The student who, according to his principal, was trying to break his gang ties. The student who had a truancy problem. The student whose stark black-and-white images on the high school wall had reflected great talent and hope—though the latter was perhaps unconscious, much as Michael had been unaware of his underlying theme of humanity until his mentor had pointed it out.

Jared Poole was exactly the kind of student David was trying to reach with Uplink. But he suspected Jared was also exactly the kind of student the board would classify as high-risk.

As David perused the application, several things became clear. Jared wasn't the strongest student. His grades were marginal, at best. Yet a letter from his art teacher praised his creativity and visual gifts. And as

David read the essay required by the application, he had to concur with the English teacher, whose enclosed assessment commended the boy's writing talent.

What he couldn't gauge from the application was Jared's determination and commitment. Much as he wanted to reach out to students like Jared, he understood—and respected—the board's wishes not to take unnecessary risks with the program at this early stage. Jared could be a great success story—or he could spell disaster. And from the pieces of paper in his hand, David couldn't tell which was more probable.

Pulling his school directory toward him, he scanned his list of principals for Charles Elliot's number, then tapped it in.

"David! Good to hear from you. I was just wondering this morning if any of our students had applied to Uplink."

"As a matter of fact, that's why I'm calling. I'm just starting to sift through the applications from all of the high schools, and one of the first ones I came across is from Jared Poole."

A couple of beats of silence ticked by before Charles spoke. "I have to say I'm surprised."

"I am, too, based on our last conversation. He doesn't fit the profile of our typical applicant. At least up until now. In any case, I wanted to take you up on your offer to give me an evaluation of students from your school who applied. How high of a risk do you think he'd be?"

Again, a few beats of silence. "If pressed, I'd have to say fifty-fifty. At best. I wish I could be more positive, but he's got a very spotty record. It's not that he doesn't have the ability to perform. When he wants to, he can apply himself. He just doesn't seem to want to most of the time."

David knew that the board members would have apoplexy if he told them he was even toying with the idea of considering such a high-risk student. "His art and English teachers included pretty strong letters of recommendation."

"Like I said, he can do great work when he's inclined to. Art and English are his two best subjects—as I'm sure you realized, if you checked the transcript required by the application."

"Yes. I saw that."

"I'd hate to be the one who derails his chances, though. With the right support and motivation, he could surprise us all."

Leaning back in his office chair, David looked out his window. The first buds of spring were just starting to come out on the flowering trees that lined the street, waiting for the warmth of the sun to coax them into blossom. Given the right conditions, and some TLC, almost any living thing could thrive. Ella's table of salvaged plants, which had withered and almost died in the hands of a variety of owners, had flourished under her care and attention. People reacted the same way. If he didn't believe that, he wouldn't have taken the job at Uplink.

With sudden decision, he turned back to his desk and pulled Jared's application toward him. "I think I'll talk to him," he told Charles.

"Good idea. You can tell a lot more in person than you can from a piece of paper."

As David hung up the phone, his face grew thoughtful. From his years of negotiating high-stakes deals, where he'd had to rely on his instincts and his ability to do a quick and accurate assessment of the players, he should have the skills to make this determination.

Then again, he hadn't had many dealings with troubled teenagers. Maybe his skills wouldn't hold up with someone like Jared.

But in his heart, he knew he had to try.

At the knock on his door, David looked up.

"Jared Poole is here." On the threshold, Ella rolled her eyes and nodded behind her.

Over her shoulder, David could see a tall, lanky teen slouched against the far wall of the reception area. When Jared looked his way, the defiance in his eyes was unmistakable. Yet David sensed the boy's nervousness beneath the cover of that brash look. Though his posture appeared relaxed, indifferent even, there was an almost palpable tension about him that told David he cared about this interview. And the fact that he'd not only shown up, but was right on time, was also a good sign.

"Thanks, Ella." As she returned to her desk, David rose and walked to the doorway. "Come in, Jared."

The boy pushed away from the wall and moved toward David, taking his time. When David offered his hand, the boy hesitated for a brief second before he took it.

"Come on in and make yourself comfortable." David gestured toward the table. "Would you like a soft drink?"

"No." As an afterthought, he tacked on a mumbled, "Thanks."

David reached for Jared's application from his desk,

then took a seat at the table beside him. With his baggy, low-slung pants, torn jacket, scuffed sneakers and dreadlocked hair, he didn't look anything like a typical Uplink applicant. David suspected that if the board were present right now, Jared would get a thumbs-down before he even had a chance to speak. But David was determined not to make any rash judgments.

"I saw some of your photographs on the wall at the school. Very impressive."

The boy shrugged. "They're okay, I guess."

"Tell me a little about your photography. How did you get involved with it?"

"I did some photos for an art project last year with a disposable camera. I guess Mrs. Thompson, the teacher, thought they were pretty good, because she let me borrow the department camera so I could do more complicated stuff."

"What kind of camera is it?"

"An old Olympus manual thirty-five millimeter. Some rich dude donated it to the school when he got tired of it."

"Who taught you to use it?"

He lifted one shoulder. "I just played around with it until I figured it out. And I've read some books about photography."

Self-taught. Impressive. "Why black-and-white instead of color?" David asked, leaning back in his chair.

"I do color, too. But black-and-white is better for… ideas."

"That's what my brother used to say."

"Is he into photography?"

"He was a photojournalist with the Associated Press. Spent years covering the world's trouble spots. He was even nominated for a Pulitzer prize once."

A flicker of interest sparked to life in Jared's eyes. "Is he still doing that?"

"No. He was killed by a suicide bomber in the Middle East while he was on assignment."

The shocked look that ricocheted across Jared's face before his mask of indifference fell back into place told David that the boy wasn't quite as thick-skinned as he tried to appear. "That's tough," he said.

"Yeah. He was very gifted."

"Is he the reason you noticed my stuff on the wall at school?"

"I guess it would be fair to say that. After Michael got involved with photography, I learned to appreciate the power of a camera in the right hands. And I learned to recognize talent." When Jared didn't seem to know how to react to that compliment, David switched gears. "Tell me why you want to be part of Uplink."

"It's all in the essay." Jared gestured to the application lying on the table in front of David.

"I want to hear it from you."

"Look, man, I'm not that good with words."

"That's not what your English teacher said in her letter of recommendation."

"Words on paper, that's okay. I don't speak words that well."

That could be true, David conceded. Some people expressed themselves better in writing—or through photos—than they did verbally. Still, he needed more from

Jared. The boy didn't exactly seem to be bubbling over with enthusiasm about the opportunities Uplink provided, and David couldn't offer an internship to someone who didn't appreciate it when dozens of others were desperate for the chance.

Pulling Jared's essay toward him, David scanned it again. It was concise and well-written, but it didn't convey compelling interest. Maybe David should let this go. Maybe he was only pursuing this because something in Jared had reminded him of Michael in his younger days. His brother had also been directionless and floundering until someone had recognized his talent and given him an entrée into the world of photography, putting him on a path that had changed his life. But once discovered, Michael's passion for photography had consumed him, his fervor so intense it was almost tangible. David wasn't sensing anything close to that in Jared. It either wasn't there, or the boy was hiding it well.

Laying the essay back down, David leveled a direct look at the young man across from him. "Let me give this to you straight, Jared. I saw something in your photography the day I was at your school that impressed me. That's why your application stood out—even though your grades overall aren't as high as those of students we've considered for this program in the past. I decided to talk with you because I respect your creative gift. But that gift isn't enough. I want students in Uplink who are passionate about the things they love to do, who have dreams and who are willing to work hard to overcome any obstacles that life might have put in their way to achieve those dreams. I look for drive and determination and commitment. I can overlook grades to some extent if all of those other things are present. But to be honest, I'm not picking up enough energy or ambition or intense motivation from you to convince me to go out on a limb and take a chance."

For several long seconds, the boy stared back at him. Indecision and defiance battled in his eyes. Defiance won.

"Hey, man, I don't need this program. Not enough to grovel." He stood and shoved his hands in his pockets, squeezing his hands into tight fists.

"I don't expect you to grovel. I just expect you to show some interest and enthusiasm. I need people who are willing to make a commitment to the program and work hard while they're in it. I couldn't tell your level of commitment from your application, but I thought I might be able to in person. I was wrong. I can't get inside your head, Jared. You're very good at masking your feelings."

The boy glared at him, his shoulders stiff. "It's called survival, man." He turned and strode toward the door, tossing a parting remark, laden with sarcasm, over his shoulder before he exited. "Thanks for your time." A few seconds later, David heard the front door open, then close.

Frustrated, David raked his fingers through his hair. All his years of experience working with hard-nosed business people hadn't helped him one iota in dealing with Jared. The boy was as tight as a clam with his feelings. Yet he had to be interested. He wouldn't have gone to the trouble of applying otherwise. But none of that came through in person. There was no way David could send a student like Jared into any of the current

Uplink hosting companies. They wouldn't put up with his attitude.

"That boy has got one big chip on his shoulder." Hands on her hips, Ella regarded him from the doorway.

"Yeah. Tell me about it."

"He's got a big hurt in his heart, too."

"Why do you say that?"

"You can see it in his eyes."

"All I saw was defiance. And suspicion."

Shaking her head, Ella folded her arms across her chest. "You've got a lot to learn about young people."

"Tell me something I don't already know." David rose and walked over to the window, then stared out at the trees. Each day, coaxed by the sun, the buds were opening a little more, revealing their inner beauty bit by bit.

"It'll come. You've got to remember that these kids aren't rich businessmen who are into power and money. Those folks are confident and they're successful. If one deal falls through, it's not a big thing. They know there's always another one coming along. A lot of the kids in the poorer neighborhoods have never tasted success. They have no confidence. All they know about life is that it stinks. They've never had a break, and even when one comes their way, they're suspicious. Why shouldn't they be? They've learned that nothing comes free. They've been conditioned to believe that they're losers. It takes a lot of guts for a kid like Jared to even take a first step like this."

"Are you saying that I should consider him for Uplink?" David turned back to her.

"That's your call. I'm just saying that maybe he wants it more than you think."

"Even if he does, I can't overlook his insolent manner. And I doubt any of our sponsoring companies could, either. They don't need or want people with attitudes. The only photography/writing slot I have available is at the *Post,* and I guarantee they wouldn't tolerate that chip on his shoulder for a day."

"Maybe you could find another place for him, with someone who's a little more tolerant and willing to take a personal interest in his development."

An image of Caroline flashed through his mind. She struck him as someone who would be willing to look deeper, who would take the time to dig through the layers of defiance and wariness to find the real Jared. Under her tutelage, the boy might blossom.

But even if he was willing to contact her again—and that was a big if—Jared still represented a major risk. Until Ella had walked into the office, he'd been prepared to write off the boy—albeit with regret. Now he wondered if he'd been too hasty.

As he pondered that, a movement down the street caught his attention. A city bus had come to a stop with a squeal of breaks, and as the doors folded open, he saw Jared disengage himself from his slouched position against one of the flowering trees and walk toward the door. His shoulders were slumped, and the confident strut he'd used in the Uplink office had become a weary shuffle. With his hands in his pockets, and his head bowed, his posture spoke of discouragement and despair. He stepped on board, the doors closed and the bus rumbled off.

All at once, the significance of what has just transpired became clear. Jared had taken a bus—probably several—to get to this interview after school. Without a car, public transportation had been the only option available to him. Yet he'd made the effort—again confirming his seriousness about the program. In fact, all of his actions spoke of his interest. It just hadn't come across in person. Yet Ella had seen something in him that he'd missed.

He turned back to the receptionist. She was still standing in the doorway, her head tilted to one side, her arms folded across her chest, her face placid and nonjudgmental. That's one of the things he liked about her. She was always willing to express her opinions, which were well thought out and insightful, but she didn't take offense if he disagreed. She respected his views, just as he respected hers.

"I think I'll give this a little more thought," he told her.

"Good idea. We always make better decisions when we think things through. Don't forget you have that conference call at five o'clock with Feldman and Associates."

"Right. Thanks." The architectural firm was considering taking an Uplink intern for the summer, and David strode toward his desk, shifting gears as he prepared to do a sell job with the management of the company. The addition of that firm would be a real plus for Uplink.

The question was, would Jared?

Lord, please give me some direction on this, David prayed as he gathered up his notes in preparation for the conference call. *I want to help Jared, but I don't want to hurt Uplink. Help me make the right decision.*

* * *

"That's a new necklace, isn't it?"

Reaching up, Caroline fingered the pewter anchor that hung on a slender chain around her neck. She'd begun wearing it on a regular basis, but she hadn't thought about her weekly dinner at her mother's home when she'd put it on this morning. If she had, she wouldn't have worn it, knowing it would prompt questions. "Yes. I gave it to Michael right before we became engaged."

"I don't remember ever seeing you wear it before."

"That's because I didn't have it until a couple of weeks ago. David dropped it off at the office. He found it among Michael's things when he was packing for his move."

"You've seen David?"

Her mother's startled reaction didn't surprise Caroline. Her meeting with David would have been a logical bit of news to share during one of their frequent phone conversations or at dinner. Caroline wasn't sure why she hadn't.

"Yes. He stopped by the *Chronicle* for a few minutes."

"Why didn't you tell me?"

"It was only a quick conversation. Nothing worth reporting." The excuse was lame, and Caroline knew it. The meeting alone would have been worthy of mention in her mother's mind.

"Of course it was! He seems like a nice young man. And I told *you* when *I* ran into him."

There was no arguing with that. "It was no big deal, Mom."

"Well…considering how you reacted when I mentioned his name a few weeks ago, I suspect it was a bigger deal than you're letting on." Her mother shoved her green beans around on her plate with more force than necessary.

Feeling guilty, Caroline tried to make amends through further disclosure. "Actually, my visit with him yesterday was more interesting."

Her mother went from miffed to curious in a heart-beat. "You've seen him twice?"

"Yes. Tess is doing a feature story about the organization he heads, and when she had a family emergency yesterday, I interviewed him in her place."

"And you weren't going to tell me?"

"I'm telling you now."

It was a hedge, but at least her mother let it pass. "So what is he doing these days?"

"He's the executive director of an organization that sets up summer internships for talented high school students from impoverished backgrounds."

"Sounds very worthwhile. But isn't that quite a switch for him? Didn't you tell me once that he was an investment banker?"

"Close. He handled merger and acquisition negotiations for multinational companies."

"What prompted the change?"

"He said it was something the Lord had called him to do."

"Then he's a religious man?" Her mother looked pleased.

"It seems so."

"Well, good for him. It's not often you hear of someone giving up a successful career to take a job for far less money, just because they think it's the right thing to do. It sounds like he has good values, and a lot of integrity."

Yes, it did sound that way, Caroline acknowledged. But she knew what he'd done to his mother. And it wasn't consistent with either of those qualities.

"You look puzzled, dear."

Her mother didn't miss a thing, that was for sure. "I'm just trying to reconcile this David with the one I met two years ago."

"Has he changed?"

Shrugging, Caroline speared a bite of pork tenderloin. "All I know is that he did something a few weeks before Michael died that doesn't seem in keeping with either good values or integrity."

"Do you want to tell me about it?"

The rift between the two brothers wasn't something Caroline had ever talked about. It had seemed too personal. But it was history now, and her mom did have good instincts. Maybe she could shed a little light on the situation that would give Caroline some new insights.

After taking a sip of water, Caroline set her glass back on the oak table in her mother's breakfast room, where so many confidences had been exchanged over the years.

"Remember I told you that Michael's mother had Alzheimer's?"

"Yes. Poor woman! What a terrible disease."

"I know. When I met Michael's mother the Christmas we got engaged, she seemed a little vague, but she was a very kind, sweet lady. I wouldn't call anything she did abnormal. But I overheard Michael and David talking about her while we were there, and Michael told me later that David wanted to break a promise they'd made to her years before and put her in an extended-care facility. Michael was upset, and I didn't blame him. At the time, she was still living on her own, and David had arranged to have someone stay with her during the day. There didn't seem to be an immediate need to take more dramatic measures."

"What happened then?"

"David agreed to wait. But a few weeks later he called Michael and reneged. They had a huge argument about it, and Michael asked him to hold off making any decision until we came home for the wedding, when they could discuss it in person. But David refused and moved ahead. They didn't talk again until the night before Michael was…before he died…when David called to say that their mother had had a mild heart attack. It was a bad situation all around."

The story had held Judy's rapt attention, and when Caroline finished her mother leaned back in her chair, a thoughtful look on her face. "Did Michael tell you why David wouldn't wait?"

"He said that according to David, we'd seen their mother on a few good days, and that she'd gotten much worse in the weeks that followed. David thought she needed constant care and was worried about leaving her alone. Not just at night, but even long enough for a caregiver to run to the grocery store or take a shower."

At Caroline's skeptical tone, Judy sent her a curious look. "And you don't believe that?"

"It doesn't matter if I believe it or not. All I know is that

Michael didn't. He knew David's career was demanding, and he figured he just didn't want to be bothered."

"That's easy to say if you're thousands of miles away and not the one who has to deal with a situation like that day after day."

Shocked, Caroline stared at her mother. "You think David was right to break the promise he and Michael made to their mother?"

"I'm not going to judge him, Caroline. All I know is that Alzheimer's patients can be a handful. Remember Rose Candici?"

Now there was a name from the past. It took Caroline a few seconds to place her. "Your high school class-mate? The one you play bridge with?"

"Yes. I never saw a woman who loved her mother more. And she had to deal with the same issue. She tried to care for her mother at home for as long as she could. They even built a self-contained suite onto their house for her, and brought in specialized care when she got worse. Rose was determined to keep her mother at home. But in the end, she needed round-the-clock care. It got to the point where she had few lucid days and no longer recognized her family. Plus, she began to have other medical problems that needed daily monitoring. The solution seemed pretty clear-cut to her friends, but Rose agonized over the decision. I'm not sure she ever reconciled herself to it."

"I don't think Michael's mother was that bad."

"Then you think David was lying?"

Caroline's reaction was immediate. No, David wouldn't lie. She didn't know him very well, but he radiated honesty—and honor. Unless her powers of intuition were way off, David was a man you could count on to do the right thing.

"I can see on your face that you don't," her mother continued, when Caroline didn't respond.

"To be honest, I don't know what to think."

Rising, Judy reached for Caroline's plate, then picked up her own. "I always believe in giving people the benefit of the doubt. That young man has caring eyes. I can't see him doing anything to hurt someone he loved. And remember…there's always at least two sides to every story. Maybe you can ask him about it sometime, if it's still on your mind. Now, how about some split lemon cake?"

It took Caroline a second to respond after the abrupt change in topic. "Sure. That would be great."

"I made it this morning. I just love the combination of tart and sweet. It's a perfect springtime dessert."

And a perfect complement to her mood, too, Caroline reflected, recalling again the events that had led to Michael's death. Even though he'd been in the marketplace because of her, she'd always believed—*wanted* to believe—that if he hadn't been distracted by his argument with his brother, he might have sensed danger. And avoided it. So for two years, she'd had tart, almost bitter, memories of David. Yet in the past couple of weeks she'd seen glimpses of sweetness, of innate goodness, that had tempered her image of him, countered her resentment and anger, mitigated the sour taste that thoughts of him usually left in her mouth.

Until now, Caroline had always assumed that Michael's position in regard to his mother had been the right one. That honor had been on his side because of his commitment to keep the vow they'd made to her. After all, Caroline had seen the woman herself mere weeks before. She couldn't have degenerated that much in such a short time.

Could she?

It wasn't a question Caroline had asked until now. She'd never allowed for the possibility that David might have made the right decision. But maybe he had. Maybe, if asked, he would explain his motivations. Her mother had even suggested she give him that opportunity.

There was just one little problem with that idea. Caroline never expected to see him again. What was the point? It just resurrected painful memories best left buried. So reaching out to him was not a good idea.

And she had the distinct impression that the feeling was mutual.

Chapter Five

"I think you'll find the letter on top very interesting."
Ella set the morning mail in David's In basket.

Focused on the computer screen in front of him,
David reread the last line in his follow-up letter to
Feldman and Associates, then sent Ella a distracted
look. "Can it wait?"

"Sure. Jared probably figures you won't respond,
anyway. Kids in that kind of environment haven't been
programmed to expect much."

Thoughts of Feldman and Associates vanished as
David stared at her. "Jared wrote me a letter?"

"Yeah. How about that? I guess maybe he was more
interested in Uplink than you thought."

Flashing her a grin, David reached for the letter.
"Thanks for not saying, 'I told you so.'"

Shrugging, she turned away. But he caught a quick
glimpse of the twinkle in her eyes. "I'll save that for
another time," she told him.

She would, too, David thought with an affectionate chuckle. Ella had been a godsend as he'd plunged into his new job, her advice sound, her insights sure. She'd become a trusted advisor and a reliable sounding board, helping to make his transition far smoother than he'd anticipated.

The letter from Jared was typed, just as his essay had been, David noted. And again, his punctuation, spelling and syntax were flawless. But as he read the text, David realized that there was one significant difference between the two writing samples. This one had heart.

Dear Mr. Sloan: After our interview yesterday, I thought about your comment that I didn't seem to have the commitment or drive or determination you look for in Uplink students. That you wanted students with dreams, who were willing to overcome any obstacles that might keep those dreams from coming true.

Well, I've had plenty of obstacles in my life. If you talked to Mr. Elliot about me, you probably know about some of them. But I figure the biggest obstacle to my success right now is me. I don't trust a lot of people. Especially white folks. And they pick that up real quick, just like you did. I know I need to change my attitude, and I'm trying. As for hard work, I'm not afraid of that. Not if it will open doors. I don't want to waste my life in the ghetto. I want to count for something, to make a difference, to leave a mark. And Uplink seems like a way to get me started on the right path. Maybe the only way.

When I left your office, though, I figured I'd blown it. That's what I told my grandmother when I got home. And she sat me down and read me the riot act about my attitude. She said if I really wanted this, I should try again. That maybe you'd give me another chance. So that's what I'm asking for, if it's not too late. I know I haven't been the best student, and that my commitment to school hasn't been as strong as you might want. But if you give me this chance, I won't disappoint you. I can work hard when I want to, and I don't break my promises. I want this opportunity very much, and if you take me, I'll give it my best shot.

Like I said when we met, I'm not very good at talking about my feelings. I guess I have to work on that, too. But for now, I hope you'll accept them in writing. And that you'll give me a second chance.

Thank you.

The letter was signed in Jared's scrawling hand.

David leaned back in his chair. He'd never expected to hear from Jared again, but the image of the dejected, slump-shouldered boy had been on his mind ever since he'd watched him get on the bus three days before. And he'd been praying for him, asking God to help Jared find a way out of his present situation, to give him an opportunity to nurture his talent. Now God had put the ball back in his court.

With sudden decision, David reached for the phone and tapped in Steve Dempsky's number. When he answered on the second ring, David gave him a quick recap of the situation, then asked for his input.

"It's a bit sticky," the minister acknowledged. "One of those things that could go either way."

"I know."

"If you brought this before the board, I doubt they'd be willing to sign Jared on."

"I know that, too. But I don't have to go to the board for this. I have the authority to choose the candidates for interviews."

"How risky do you think this is? Could he jeopardize the program?"

Leaning back in his chair, David looked out at the flowering trees. "That's the sixty-four-thousand-dollar question. I do know he's exactly the kind of student who needs Uplink the most."

"What does your gut tell you about the risk?"

"Three days ago, after I interviewed him, I'd have said it was high. He has a real attitude problem that I knew none of our sponsoring companies would put up with. I'd more or less written him off. Then, when I saw him getting on the bus, he was the picture of dejection. And today I got the letter. I think he wants this, Steve. And I know he needs it."

"Would you like me to talk to him?"

"I was hoping you'd offer. I know it's still my decision, and I'll take full responsibility for it, but I'd value your input."

"Glad to help. Just have him give me a call."

"Thanks, buddy."

"Hey, what are friends for?"

As David replaced the receiver, a sense of peace came over him. He still wasn't sure what his decision would be. But he knew he would do everything he could to give the boy a chance. That's what Uplink was supposed to be about. If Steve concurred that Jared was worth the risk, David would take it. And put the outcome in God's hands.

"You want me to talk to a preacher?"

From the tone of Jared's voice, you'd think he'd asked the boy to walk over hot coals barefoot, David reflected, a wry smile touching his lips. Their phone conversation had started off well enough, although Jared had seemed surprised that David had followed up on his letter. It was as if he'd expected nothing from the effort. Or hadn't allowed himself to expect anything. Just as Ella had suggested. But at least his tone had been cordial, and it had been obvious that he was making an attempt to keep his attitude in check. Until David mentioned Steve.

"That's right," David affirmed. "He's a member of the Uplink board and an old friend of mine. I value his opinion, and when he offered to speak with you I took him up on it."

"Do you send all the Uplink candidates to talk to him?"

"No." David decided that absolute honesty was the best way to proceed with Jared. He suspected the boy would respect that in the long run. "But your situation is a bit unique. In general, we wouldn't consider someone with your GPA or attendance record. But as I said when we spoke before, I'm impressed with your talent. I think you have a lot to offer, assuming you buckle down. Your letter makes me think you're willing to do that. But I want a second opinion."

There was silence for a few seconds before Jared responded. "I'm not a religious kind of person."

"Religion isn't on the agenda for your meeting with Reverend Dempsky."

"Then what's he going to ask me about?"

"A lot of the same things I did."

"And he won't get into that Jesus stuff?"

"No. Uplink isn't a Christian organization, even though it lives the gospel principles."

There was a moment of silence while Jared thought about that. "Yeah, okay. I guess that's fine. When does he want to talk to me?"

"You two can work that out. Just give him a call." David recited Steve's number while Jared jotted it down.

"What happens after that?"

David heard the anxious note in the boy's voice. "We'll be notifying all of the finalists by May first. There will be one more interview after that, with the sponsoring organization. The internships run ten weeks and start in early June. Do you have a portfolio of writing and photography samples, Jared?"

"No."

"Put one together. It doesn't have to be fancy. Just a collection of some of your best work. And include copies of the letters from your English and art teachers. I'd like you to show it to Reverend Dempsky, and you'll need it for an interview with a sponsoring organization if we get that far."

"Okay."

"Any other questions?"

"No."

"All right. I'll talk to you soon, then."

"Listen…thanks, okay? I—I didn't really expect you to give me a second chance."

That comment probably summed up the breadth of the boy's experience, David thought with a pang. "Everyone deserves a second chance, Jared."

"A lot of people don't feel that way."

"Well, Uplink does. Just make the most of it, okay?"

As David rang off, he wasn't sure the board would agree with him about second chances. Not when it came to someone like Jared, who could be a high risk. But Michael had been a risk, too, when a mentor had stepped forward and taken a chance on him. It was something Michael had never forgotten, and he'd vowed someday to repay that debt by helping another young person. In the end, he'd never had the opportunity to follow through on that pledge. His life had been cut way too short, and despite Caroline's confession, David still felt somewhat responsible for that. Perhaps, by fulfilling Michael's vow for him, he could in some way make amends for any role he'd played in his brother's death.

Still, he wasn't going to take unnecessary chances or let his judgment be clouded by personal feelings. He had to do what was right for Uplink. But if Steve considered Jared to be a worthy candidate, David would take the boy on in a second.

"David? Steve. Got a few minutes?"

This was it. Jared was on spring break, and David knew Steve had met with him earlier in the day. His grip on the phone tightened, and the muscles in his shoulders bunched. "Yeah. How did it go?"

"Let me just say that I can see why you wanted a second opinion."

Uh-oh. Not good. "You weren't impressed?"

"I didn't say that. He's got talent, no question about it. He brought along a very impressive portfolio. But I picked up on the attitude, even though it was clear he was trying to keep it in check. Plus, I think he was very uncomfortable with the whole notion of talking to a minister. I tried to put him at ease, but I sensed a lot of wariness and suspicion."

That sounded like Jared. "Anything else?"

"Yeah. His appearance. I could live with the dreadlocks. But I can't see most of the organizations we work with allowing that kind of attire. Most of them have dress codes, and even though casual clothes are okay at a lot of places, his concept of casual falls way below that line. I know the Lord teaches us not to judge by appearances, but most businesses aren't that forgiving."

"We could work with him on that."

"True."

"Well, what do you think? Yea or nay on letting him into the program?"

"It's not an easy call, is it?"

David could hear the uncertainty in his friend's voice. "No."

"I guess you're just going to have to go with your heart on this one. I do think Jared wants this. But I also think he's a risk. I talked with him a little about his gang ties, and he claims he's cutting those, like his principal told you. That's hard to do, though, and there's no guarantee of success. And what if he gets into the program and then loses interest halfway through? Or can't get along with his coworkers? Or does something worse? Did you check to see if he has a juvenile record?"

"Yeah. Charles Elliot, his principal, says he's had a few minor brushes with the law, but there's nothing on record. At this point, he's officially clean."

"Well, that's good news, at least."

David had hoped for a definitive opinion from Steve. But his friend's feelings seemed as mixed as his own.

"What did you think of the photos?"

"Like I said, impressive. Even though the images are stark, there's a certain optimistic quality to them that suggests…goodness, maybe. They make me think there's a light deep in his soul, waiting to be released. Frankly, without the photos I suspect I'd write him off as too risky. But those pictures tugged at my heart."

So Steve had noticed that, too. David had made it a point to keep his impressions about the photos to himself, wondering if Steve would pick up on the same qualities he had, qualities that not only reflected Jared's good eye for photography but also offered a window into his soul. Qualities that suggested the boy wasn't quite as jaded as he might first appear, that there was a chance he could make something of his life, with assistance. The kind of assistance Uplink offered.

"They had the same effect on me," David responded.

"What are you going to do?"

"Think about it. And pray."

"Sounds like a good plan. I'll support whatever decision you make."

"Thanks."

"Just one question. Where would you place him if you decide to take him on? I can't think of any organization on our roster that would help him develop his writing and photography talent. Or take the time to give him the kind of personal attention I suspect he'll need."

Until now, David hadn't let himself dwell on that issue. He'd been too busy to worry about a problem that might never materialize. But Steve was right. He needed to start thinking about lining up a spot for Jared if he was getting serious about taking the boy.

"The *Post* might work, but it's such a big organization that I doubt he'd get the kind of one-on-one assistance he may need to blossom. I'll have to find a new place," David responded.

"It's getting pretty late in the year to start recruiting new businesses."

"I know." In the end, the decision to take Jared might come down to whether they could find somewhere to place him.

"Well, let me know what you decide. Like I said, I'm with you either way."

"Thanks, Steve. I'll be in touch."

As David replaced the phone, he'd already decided that Jared was a risk he was willing to take—if he could find a place where the boy would receive the kind of attention and support he would need to succeed. That was a big if. Most businesses were too busy to devote a lot of attention to a student intern. And too many of them just gave the teenagers busy work. David had addressed that issue with the offending organizations on Uplink's roster after reading evaluations by previous participants. That had been the single biggest complaint by students, who were anxious to spread their wings and be exposed to new experiences. A few organizations hadn't lived up to their end of the bargain.

But Jared's case was even more difficult. He not only needed exposure to the business world, but step-by-step guidance. And someone who believed in his potential.

David was too new in town to have a lot of contacts yet. He was still making the rounds of area businesses, selling in the program, meeting the right people, answering questions. He couldn't just pick up the phone and secure the perfect spot for Jared.

Or could he?

"Caroline, I have David Sloan on the line for you. Do you want to take the call?"

Surprised, Caroline stared at the thank-you note from David on her desk, expressing his appreciation for the story that had run earlier in the week about Uplink. Tess had received a similar note. Though few people bothered with such niceties after the *Chronicle* ran a story, she hadn't been surprised when David's handwritten note arrived. It had just seemed like something he would do.

But she *was* surprised by his call. With the story finished and his note sent, she'd expected that to be the end of their contact. Had hoped it would be, in fact. She still found it difficult to deal with him. And was disturbed by the questions that his reappearance in her life had raised. It had been easy to paint him as the villain in the dilemma with his mother when all she had to go on was Michael's angry assessment of the situation. It had been a whole lot harder to reconcile the living, breathing man, who exuded character and integrity and honor, with the uncaring, selfish portrait of him that Michael had painted in his fury after David had reneged on their promise.

Of course, that was all over now. The rift between the brothers was history. It didn't much matter who had been right and who had been wrong. Yet every time she heard from David, the questions were stirred up in Caroline's mind. Had she been too harsh in her judgment of David? Had she been unfair in accepting Michael's judgment at face value? And at this point, why should she care? Caroline didn't have the answer to any of those questions, especially the last one. And she wasn't even sure she wanted to find them. That's why she preferred to cut all contact with David.

"Caroline?"

"Sorry, Mary. I got distracted for a minute." She could refuse his call. But that wasn't a very mature way to behave, she supposed. She'd had the distinct feeling that he hadn't intended to contact her again, either. If he was doing so, there must be a good reason. She might as well talk to him. "Okay, put him through."

After her greeting, his voice came over the line. "Thanks for taking my call, Caroline. I know you're busy."

"No problem. What can I do for you?"

"I have an idea I'd like to run by you, if you could spare a few minutes."

She glanced at her watch. "I've got about ten minutes now, if that works."

"I'd prefer to do this in person. There's a show-and-tell component."

"Is this personal or business related?"

She didn't try to disguise the wariness in her voice. Nor did he miss it.

"Business." His reply was prompt and definite.

The tautness in Caroline's shoulders eased. Curiosity replaced tension, and she reached for her calendar. As usual, almost every second of her day was booked. She flipped to the next week. Not much better. But she had one open slot late on Thursday.

"How about April thirtieth at three o'clock?"

A frown creased David's brow. That was pushing it. Finalists were scheduled to be notified by May first and interviewed the following week at sponsoring businesses. "Is there any way you can squeeze me in sometime this week? I'm sorry to push, but this is important and there's some urgency due to our deadlines."

Flipping back the calendar, Caroline scanned her schedule as she spoke. "Do you want to give me a hint what this is about?"

No, he didn't. David knew from experience that it was too easy for people to say no over the phone. He wanted Caroline to see Jared's work before she made a decision. But her question was legitimate. In her place, he'd ask the same thing. Time was at a premium in most jobs.

"I have an unusual Uplink applicant whose talent has blown me away. I'd like to get a second opinion before I try to place him, and his skills are in your area of expertise. Since I'm new in town, you're the only journalist I know well enough to call." Okay, that wasn't the whole truth. But he'd rather press his case for the *Chronicle*'s involvement in person.

"Okay. I can do that." She scanned her schedule again, doing some rapid mental rearranging. She'd planned to run a couple of errands over lunch tomorrow, but they could be deferred. "I've got about forty-five minutes tomorrow at noon. Would that work?"

"Only if you let me buy you lunch."

She seemed surprised by the invitation. But no more than he was. Since he'd planned to keep this strictly business, introducing a social component wasn't a good idea.

"That's not necessary," she assured him.

"At least let me bring some sandwiches."

"Really, David, you don't have to do that."

"Would turkey be okay?"

He wasn't going to relent, she realized. Besides, it wasn't that big a deal. She should eat lunch, anyway. If he didn't bring food, though, she knew she'd skip. Again. She'd never regained the weight she'd lost after Michael's death, and her mother was always on her about eating more.

"Turkey's fine. Thanks. About noon?"

"I'll be there. I appreciate your time, Caroline."

"No problem. See you tomorrow."

No problem. The words echoed in his mind as he hung up. Maybe not for her. But seeing Caroline again was a big problem for him, given his feelings for her. Only a compelling need to help Jared would have prompted him to make another contact. To take that risk. And risk was the right word—one that had been on his mind a lot in recent weeks, thanks to Jared. Taking a chance on the troubled teenager put Uplink in a high-risk situation. Not to mention the risk he was taking professionally. If things didn't work out, his new career could be toast.

But all at once that risk paled in comparison to the one he was taking on a personal level by seeing Caroline again. Because when it came to his emotions, he was on dangerous ground with her. And he felt far less confident about controlling *that* risk.

Chapter Six

"Caroline, David Sloan is here."

Shifting the phone to her other ear, Caroline reached for a pad of paper and a pen. "Thanks, Mary. Can you show him to the conference room? Tell him I'll be with him as soon as I return a call."

"Sure thing."

By the time Caroline joined him a few minutes later, David had unpacked the lunch and eating utensils, and set a three-ring binder on the table. He rose as she entered and held out his hand, taking her slender fingers in a firm grip.

"Sorry to keep you waiting. I had to return an urgent call," she apologized.

"I'm just glad you could squeeze me in." He waited until she took her seat, then sat as well. "There's a little deli near my office that makes a great turkey on whole wheat. I picked up a few other things, too."

Surveying the containers of pasta salad, potato salad

and fresh fruit salad—not to mention brownies—Caroline shook her head. "This is more than I eat for lunch in a week."

"You can afford to indulge."

As she reached for her sandwich, she angled a bemused look his way. "Now you sound like my mother. She's always on me about my weight."

"You do look thinner than I remember."

Her hand stilled on the plastic wrap for a fraction of a second before she continued to unwrap her sandwich. "Life keeps me busy. Sometimes too busy to take time for meals. But I have a healthy appetite when I do eat." As if to illustrate her point, she took a big bite of her sandwich, then scooped a large serving of pasta salad onto her plate. "Is this the work of the student you mentioned?" She nodded toward the portfolio as she chewed.

"Yes. Jared Poole. I saw some of his photographs on the wall when I did a presentation at his school, and later found out he's a talented writer as well. But he isn't a typical Uplink candidate. He has gang ties, which he's trying to break, and is only a marginal student overall. He also has a truancy issue. Not to mention an attitude problem. The chip on his shoulder is more like a boulder."

Tilting her head, Caroline gave him a puzzled look. "With all those negatives, why are you considering him? The gang connection in particular is troubling."

"I agree. But without help, his future looks pretty bleak. His father disappeared before he was born, his mother died of a drug overdose when he was a little kid and he's being raised by a grandmother who has to clean office buildings at night just to keep food on the table.

From what I can tell, no one's ever given him a break. Uplink could make a huge difference in his life."

"Maybe. But he sounds risky."

"He is."

Her perceptive hazel eyes missing nothing, Caroline scrutinized his face. "There's more behind your interest, isn't there?"

Instead of giving her a direct response, David slid the portfolio closer to her. "Take a look."

Wiping her hands on a napkin, Caroline opened the binder. Writing and photo samples had been slipped into plastic sheets, and she took her time reviewing each one. The minutes slipped by, and David continued to eat, watching in silence as she gave her full attention to the material in Jared's folder.

She spent a long time examining the three photos that had first caught David's attention, and when she at last closed the binder and looked over at him, he could see that she was impressed even before she voiced her single-word assessment.

"Wow."

"That's what I thought. But I'm not an expert."

"How old is he?"

"Seventeen."

She shook her head. "His writing is very good. But the photos...they're exceptional."

"Now you can see why I didn't want to let him slip through the cracks. A talent like his needs to be nurtured."

"I agree."

"Here's the issue, though." David wiped his lips on a paper napkin and leaned forward, his face intent as he folded his hands on the table in front of him. "Taking Jared on would require a huge commitment from the sponsoring organization. He's going to need personal attention and understanding and patience. He'll need to be challenged and held accountable. That's assuming we find an organization that recognizes his talents and can put them to good use."

As Caroline gazed into David's serious, deep brown eyes, a wry smile touched the corners of her lips—even as her heart did an odd flip-flop that threw her off balance for a brief instant. "I think I'm beginning to see why you offered to buy me lunch."

"Not that you've eaten any of it." David was well aware that she'd taken only a couple of bites of her sandwich and a forkful of pasta salad before she'd become absorbed in Jared's portfolio.

"This happens all the time. There are way too many interruptions at the office to make take-out worthwhile. But this is really good." She reached for her sandwich and took another bite.

"So…what do you think? Would you even consider taking Jared for the summer? Assuming you wanted him after an interview, of course."

Her face grew speculative as she chewed, and she sipped her soda before responding. "We've never hired an intern. They tend to require significant training time from a staff already stretched too thin. And just when we start to get some productivity out of them, the internship ends."

"I understand those concerns. It's no great bargain for the sponsoring organizations, although the students do work for minimum wage, so it's not a big financial commitment. But it does require staff time from one or two people. We like students to be assigned to a mentor or two who can guide them through the process and make sure they're getting the most out of the experience. The rewards for the student are incalculable, though."

Once more, Caroline opened the portfolio to the black-and-white photos. Her face softened as she studied them, her lunch once again forgotten. "Michael once told me about the mentor who recognized his talent and set him on the right path. He always talked about how much he owed him, and how he wanted to do the same someday for some other young person."

She turned to the next page, to the photo of the two children looking toward the sky. "Jared's photos make me think of Michael," she continued, and the quiet wistfulness in her voice tightened David's throat. "Even though there's a desolation to them, something shines through that touches my heart. Michael's photos made me think of the preciousness of each individual life. These make me think of aspirations and hopes and dreams."

When she looked up, the pensive expression on David's face made her suspect that the parallels hadn't been lost on him, either.

"I thought the same thing," he confirmed, after clearing his throat.

"So are you doing this for Jared? Or for Michael?"

He hesitated, then gave her an honest answer. "Maybe both."

Indecision flickered in her eyes, and David prayed she'd at least consider taking Jared on.

"Let me think about it. I'd also like to share Jared's work with our chief photographer, Bill Baker. He'd be the logical mentor on the photography side. Can I get back to you tomorrow with an answer?"

"Sure." He'd hoped for an affirmative response today. But at least she hadn't said no.

Checking her watch, Caroline rose. "I'm sorry to run, but I have an interview at one and I need to prep."

David stood as well and began gathering up the remnants of their lunch. "I understand. I appreciate your giving up your lunch hour to see me."

"And I appreciate the lunch."

"You didn't eat much of it."

Reaching for her sandwich, she rewrapped it. "I'll finish this later."

"I'll leave the rest, too."

"Thanks. My mother would love that pasta salad. And I'm going to see her tonight."

"Perfect. Give her my best." David held out his hand. "I'll wait to hear from you."

She took it, and as his lean fingers closed around hers and their gazes met, her heart did that funny flip-flop thing again. He had wonderful eyes, she realized. Warm and insightful and caring. And his grip was sure and strong, yet gentle and comforting. By look and by touch, he made her feel protected and cherished. Did he have this effect on everyone? she wondered, feeling a bit dazed.

As they stared at each other, Caroline sensed an almost imperceptible tightening of his grip. A flash of something she couldn't identify ricocheted through his eyes, come and gone with such speed that she wondered if she'd imagined it. Then, with a move that startled her by its abruptness, David released her hand and took a step back.

"I hope you find time to finish that." He gestured toward the sandwich she was clutching in her hand. With a brief nod, he turned away and strode out of the conference room.

For a full minute, Caroline stared after him, trying to figure out what had just happened. Whatever had flared to life in David's eyes had made her heart trip into double time, and for a brief second she'd felt...attracted to him. But that was impossible. She'd resented him for two years. Besides, he was the brother of the man she'd loved. The man she *still* loved. She shouldn't feel anything for him except friendship. *Couldn't* feel anything. It would be wrong. A betrayal of Michael. Of their love. Whatever had just happened must have been simply a fluke. And no doubt she'd read far too much into it.

Even so, discussing his visit with her mother wasn't going to be easy. And she refused to consider why.

"This is great pasta salad! A perfect accompaniment to our first barbecue of the year." Caroline's mother, Judy, helped herself to another serving as the sun dipped behind the trees at the back of the yard, dimming the light on the brick patio.

"I'm glad you like it." Before her mother could comment further, Caroline switched topics. "Now tell me how the square dancing lessons are going. Is Harold catching on?"

"He's trying, let me just say that. And you have to

give a man credit for trying." She took a closer look at the pasta salad. "I think there's avocado in here. Where did you get this?"

Caroline took a deep breath and plunged in. "I had a meeting at noon with David Sloan today. He brought lunch. This was left over."

Judy stared at her daughter, the pasta salad now forgotten. "You met with David again?"

"Yes. He wants the *Chronicle* to take an Uplink intern for the summer."

"Are you going to?"

"I don't know yet. This particular student has problems. And it takes a lot of staff time to deal with an intern."

"But time well spent, I would think, from what you've told me about Uplink."

It was hard to argue with that. "I gave Bill the student's portfolio. I want to see what he thinks about his potential."

"What kind of problems does this student have?"

As Caroline gave her a brief overview, Judy shook her head. "It makes you appreciate your own blessings when you hear a story like that. The boy sounds like he could use a break."

Tracing the ring of moisture left by her water glass on the patio table, Caroline's face grew melancholic. "His situation reminds me a lot of Michael's. Not the upbringing. But the raw talent, just waiting to be recognized and directed."

"Maybe that's what caught David's attention, too."

Her mother's insight never failed to surprise Caroline. Despite her sometimes flighty ways, she had a keen sense of human nature. "I think you're right."

"You know, it must be hard on him."

Confused, Caroline gave her mother a puzzled look. "What do you mean?"

"I was just thinking how alone David is. He had no one to comfort him when Michael died. Now he has no family left, he's living in a strange new town where he probably hasn't had much chance to make friends and he's trying to learn a new job. You should ask him to join us sometime for our weekly dinner."

Speechless, Caroline stared at her mother.

"Why do you look so surprised?" Judy asked. "It would be an act of Christian charity to invite him. Mentioning his name doesn't seem to upset you, like it did a few weeks ago when I told you I'd run into him, or I wouldn't even suggest it. And it might give you a chance to ask him about that situation with his mother, which seems to bother you."

"It doesn't bother me. It's ancient history. Why should it bother me?"

"I didn't say it should. Just that it seems to. But that's up to you, of course. In the meantime, tell him I enjoyed his pasta salad."

Her mother moved on to a new topic, and even though Caroline tried to keep up, thoughts of David kept disrupting her concentration. The fact was, the disagreement between the brothers did bother her, history or not. And somewhere, deep inside, she wanted to hear David's story, sensing at some intuitive level that it might absolve him from guilt. Why that was important to her, she had no idea. In fact, if David had been right, that would mean Michael had been wrong. Why would she want to believe that? And why did it matter at this point, anyway?

There were no easy answers to those questions. Nor were they ones Caroline necessarily wanted to find. Because she had the oddest sense that if she delved deeper, if she heard David's side of the story, she would have to rethink and reevaluate a whole lot of things. And she wasn't sure she was ready to do that.

"This kid has talent." Bill Baker strode into Caroline's office without knocking, plopped Jared's portfolio on her desk and sat in the chair across from her.

"Have a seat, Bill." She smiled as she reached for the portfolio.

Social nuances were lost on the brusque, craggy-faced photographer. With his shaggy white hair pulled back in an elastic band, his startling blue eyes rimmed with fine lines and his standard attire of blue jeans and T-shirt, he wasn't a typical *Chronicle* staff member. He didn't waste time on office politics, and tact wasn't his strong suit. But he had a heart of gold. Not to mention the best photographic skills in the business. The newspaper was lucky to have him.

"Do you have time to work with him if we decide to take him on?"

"I can make time. But I can't help him much on the writing end."

Caroline had already thought about that. And decided that she'd mentor him in writing if they proceeded. They'd lost a couple of people through attrition in the past few months, and the top brass in the parent organization had made the decision not to replace them. She couldn't ask any of her busy staffers to take on yet another responsibility. Besides, from her conversations with David, she understood that Jared was a high risk. She wanted to give this her best shot if she decided to take him on.

"I'll handle that. Do you have any concerns about the issues he has?" She'd already given Bill an overview of Jared's background.

"Some. But if he's willing to work hard, I'm willing to give him a chance."

"Okay. I'll set up an interview."

Rising, Bill nodded toward the portfolio on Caroline's desk. "I'd hate to see a talent like that go to waste. And I like challenges." Without giving her time to respond, he exited.

As Caroline watched him leave, she hoped they wouldn't live to regret Bill's words. She liked challenges, too. But she had a feeling that Jared Poole was going to be a bigger challenge than either of them imagined.

What in the world had David been thinking?

Caroline stared in dismay at the young man who took his time rising when she stepped into the lobby to greet him for the interview. Jared's low-slung pants, scuffed sneakers, muscle shirt and dreadlocks made Bill's appearance look preppy. Tall and lanky, his complexion the color of rich café au lait, he had dark, brazen eyes that stared back at her with a bravado she suspected was more wishful than real.

But she tried to keep an open mind. If David thought

Jared had the right stuff, if he was willing to take a chance and put his career on the line for this young man, Caroline at least owed him the benefit of the doubt. Summoning up a smile, she moved toward him and extended her hand.

"Jared, I'm Caroline James. Welcome to the *Chronicle*."

After a brief hesitation, he rubbed his palm on his thigh, then took her hand. She thought she detected a slight tremor in his fingers, but he retrieved his hand and shoved it in his pocket before she could tell for sure.

"Thanks," he mumbled.

"Come on back to the conference room. Bill Baker, our chief photographer, is waiting." She held her ID card to the scanner, then led the way into the newsroom. Jared followed close behind her, giving the beehive of activity around him a discreet, but interested, perusal.

At the door to the glass-walled conference room, Caroline paused. "Can I get you a soda?"

"No. Thanks." The latter was tacked on as an afterthought.

"Okay. Then let's get started."

After she introduced him to Bill, they all took seats at the long table, Caroline at the head, Bill on one side, Jared on the other. Jared's portfolio lay in the center.

For the first few minutes, Caroline kept the conversation general. But it was like pulling teeth to get the boy to open up. The writing in his portfolio and the letter David had shared with her showed a different side of Jared than he was revealing in the interview. And the attitude David had spoken of was very apparent. An attitude that screamed, "Why would you do this for me and what's in it for you?" A kaleidoscope of emotions—suspicion, anxiety, belligerence and longing—shifted across the face of the rigid-shouldered young man sitting beside her, his hands tightly clasped on the table in front of him. She suspected he was trying to control his attitude, trying to sort through his jumbled feelings, but he was having limited success.

Since small talk wasn't putting the boy at ease, Caroline decided to plunge right into the guts of the interview. "Okay, let's talk about the internship, Jared. You're here because David Sloan believes in you, and because he and I and Bill all agree that you have talent. We're sure that if you apply yourself, you can succeed. What we're not sure about is whether you'll do that. If we bring you on board, we think there's a risk. David seems convinced that it's a risk worth taking. We need you to convince us of that, too."

He swallowed. "I want to do this."

"Tell us why we should give you this chance when there are a dozen other students we could take who have better grades and better attendance records."

He swallowed again. Hard. "Look, I don't want to spend my life in the ghetto. And this may be my best chance to get out. I'll try hard not to disappoint anyone. I like working with words and I…I love photography. But I need help to get better at both. The kind of help I can get through Uplink."

"Do you still have gang ties?" It was the first question Bill had asked.

"I'm working on breaking them."

"Work harder. What about drugs? You'll have to take a drug test to work here. Standard procedure."

The boy stiffened. "I'm clean."

"Good. Keep it that way. You'll have to do something about your clothes, too. There's a dress code here. Not that you'd know it, looking at me."

Jared turned to Caroline, elegant as always in a slim black skirt, silk blouse and gold necklace. "I don't have fancy clothes."

"You don't need fancy clothes. Bill's at one end of the clothes spectrum. I'm at the other. Some of that is by necessity. Bill's work out in the field takes him to places that aren't always conducive to nicer clothes. Jeans allow him to climb on walls, get down on the ground, do whatever it takes to get the shots he needs. The important thing to remember is that journalists or photographers never call attention to themselves. We strive to blend in. The focus should be on the subjects, and we need to do everything possible to make them feel comfortable so that we can get the best story or the best photo. We can work on the clothes, as long as you're agreeable."

"Yeah. I guess so."

"Okay. I'll want you to do a writing test before you leave. That's also standard practice for new hires. We'll give you some facts, and ask you to write a story. I'll set you up at one of the empty workstations when we're done here. Bill, anything you want to ask about first?"

"Just a few technical things." He pulled Jared's portfolio toward him and flipped it open to the photo of the two shadows. "Tell me a little about this. Why you framed it this way, what kind of lighting you used, why you chose this angle."

As the two of them discussed the photo, Caroline leaned back and observed. Jared became more animated the longer they conversed, and she saw something flicker to life in his eyes. Something she'd seen in Michael's eyes as he talked about his work. Passion. Excitement. Conviction. It wasn't as easy to spot in Jared. He'd learned to mask his feelings. But it was there. His eyes might be hard, but they weren't yet calcified. Meaning there was hope for him.

When Bill was finished, Caroline settled Jared into a workstation and gave him the material for a story. Once she was sure he understood the word processing program, she stood. "Take your time. When you're finished just knock on my door. I'm right over there." She gestured toward her office near the back wall.

Half an hour later, Jared appeared at her door, his portfolio tucked under his arm. "I'm done." He took a step into her office and handed over two double-spaced sheets of text.

"Great." She scanned the first couple of lines, impressed by the lead. The piece looked promising. "That wraps it up, then. Let me walk you out." She set the sheets on her desk and led the way to the front. If the rest of the article looked as good as the lead, she was pretty sure she was going to take him on—pending Bill's agreement, of course. This was going to have to be a team effort.

After pushing through the door to the lobby, she turned to shake hands with the teenager. "Thanks for coming in, Jared. Bill and I appreciate your time. I'm sure David Sloan will be in touch with you soon."

He wanted to ask more. She could read the question in his eyes. But she didn't have an answer for him. Not yet. Besides, it wasn't her place to tell him the outcome. However, it took all of her willpower to keep her expression placid, when she could see the yearning on his face.

"Yeah. No problem." He returned her handshake. Then, after hesitating a moment, he swaggered to the door. As if to say, I have my pride. I don't need you. I'm just fine on my own.

But Caroline knew otherwise. So did David. And in his heart, she suspected Jared did, too.

She just hoped he was smart enough to recognize that Uplink was the opportunity of a lifetime and to follow through on his promise to give it his best shot.

Chapter Seven

"Jared? David Sloan. You're in."

Several beats of silence ticked by on the other end of the line before Jared responded. "For real?"

"Yeah. For real."

"Okay, man. That's good."

Although the teenager was trying to sound cool, David could hear the undercurrent of excitement in his voice. "I'll send you an official letter, but I figured you'd want to know right away."

"Yeah."

"There's a meeting for all of the participating students and their mentors from the sponsoring organizations a week from Saturday, from nine to eleven. The details are in the letter, but I just wanted to give you a heads-up."

"I'll be there."

"Any questions in the meantime?"

"No."

"If you think of any, don't hesitate to call me. We'll look forward to having you in the program, Jared. Caroline James and Bill Baker were impressed with your talent, and they'll both be serving as mentors for you at the *Chronicle*. They'll be at the meeting."

"Okay." He hesitated, then tacked on a single word before breaking the connection. "Thanks."

As David hung up, he found Ella regarding him from his office doorway, a pleased look on her face. "You took him."

"Yes. After a lot of soul-searching. But I still think he's a risk. I'll be praying that he recognizes this for the fabulous opportunity it is and takes advantage of it."

"He strikes me as a smart young man. And Caroline James impresses me as a very caring, compassionate person. Working with her, I think he'll do fine."

"You just met each of them one time. Do you always jump to conclusions based on first impressions?"

Shrugging, she laid some correspondence in his In basket. "Don't discount first impressions. It doesn't take long to pick up people's vibes, if you listen with your heart. And kindness can produce amazing results."

As she exited, David swiveled toward his window, his face thoughtful. The trees had now been coaxed into full and glorious bloom by the warmth of the spring sun. Though they'd looked dead and lifeless a month ago, under nurturing conditions they had flourished.

David prayed the same would be true for Jared.

The meeting room at Matejka Industries was packed with Uplink students and their mentors. Stefan Matejka, a Bosnian immigrant who was one of Uplink's biggest supporters, had donated the use of his facilities for the orientation meeting, as he had since Uplink's inception. Thanks to the generosity of people like him, Uplink was beginning to establish a strong foothold in the community.

As David surveyed the room, he recognized the students he'd interviewed over the past month. All had been eager, interested and grateful for the opportunity, and he could feel the excitement and electricity in the room. It was a good feeling—one he'd never experienced in his previous career. Yes, there had been satisfaction when he'd closed a deal. But once he'd walked out the door, he'd forgotten about it. It was business. His work had involved dollars, not lives. It had made no lasting contribution to society. This job, in contrast, was about people. About recognizing talent and ability, and finding ways to nurture it. It was about changing lives for the better. Most of all, it was about hope.

Once more, David scanned the crowd. Almost every seat was filled. Even the board was on hand. The expectant faces turned his way reminded him that it was time to begin. But there was one little problem.

Jared was nowhere to be seen.

When David spotted Caroline, seated with Bill about halfway back, she sent him a questioning look. He gave a slight shake of his head and lifted his shoulders. As he watched, she leaned toward Bill, said a few words then rose and made her way toward him. He met her at the side of the raised platform, and as he leaned down she spoke.

"I take it you have no idea where Jared is?"

"No." Once more David surveyed the room, a frown marring his brow. "I knew he was a risk, but I didn't expect him to go AWOL this soon." Sighing, he raked his fingers through his hair. "There's no reason for the two of you to stay if he doesn't show."

"Maybe he just got delayed. We'll hang around for a while. Do you want me to try calling him?"

"If you wouldn't mind, that would be great." He checked his watch. "I need to get started, or I'd do it myself. Ella has all the students' numbers with her. She's probably still at the registration table."

"Okay. I'll give it a try."

Ten minutes later, Caroline reappeared and slipped into her seat. She mouthed "no answer" when he looked her way. An hour later, at the break, David tried himself—with the same result.

"Look, I hate to waste your time," he told Bill and Caroline before he went back to the front to resume the meeting. "If you need to take off, I understand."

"You'll be wrapping up in forty-five minutes. I'll hang around," Bill said.

"Me, too," Caroline added. "Maybe there's a good explanation for Jared's absence today. If he's still going to participate, Bill and I need to be part of this orientation."

"All right. Thanks."

By the time the meeting broke up, Jared had still not appeared. David was kept busy answering questions from mentors and students for another fifteen minutes. By then, the crowd had dispersed. Bill had left, but Caroline was still sitting off to one side, talking on her cell phone as Ella collected the stray printed material in the chairs and on the information table.

David approached Caroline, waiting while she finished her conversation. Then she stood, dropping her phone into her tote. "Sorry. A bit of a crisis at the *Chronicle*."

"No problem. I appreciate that you and Bill stayed for the whole thing." He shook his head. "I just can't figure this out. Jared promised he'd be here when I spoke with him, and I thought he was sincere. Either my judgment is way off base, or something's wrong."

"Why don't you try him one more time before I leave? I'm a little worried myself."

"Are you sure you don't mind waiting?"

"I've invested this much time. Another couple of minutes won't hurt."

"Okay." He withdrew his cell phone and hit redial, hoping for an answer but not really expecting one. When a woman's voice came over the line, his face registered surprise. "Hello. Is Jared there?"

After a couple of seconds, she responded in a cautious tone. "Yes. But he can't come to the phone right now."

The woman had to be Jared's grandmother. Her voice sounded older—and a bit fearful, David noted. He'd seen her name on Jared's application, and he searched his memory, trying to call it up. Grace. Grace Morris.

"Ms. Morris? This is David Sloan from Uplink. We had an orientation meeting this morning for our new student interns, and we were concerned when Jared didn't attend. I wanted to follow up and make sure everything was okay."

Again, a hesitation. "No, Mr. Sloan, I'm afraid it's not. Jared had a…a run-in with his former gang last night."

Twin furrows appeared on David's brow. "Is he all right?"

"I'm taking care of him. But I'm afraid he's going to have to drop out of the program."

Whatever had happened last night must have been worse than she was letting on. "We'd hate to lose him, Ms. Morris. He's a very talented young man."

"I know. And I'm very sorry that he's going to miss this opportunity. But I think it's…better…this way."

Safer was what she meant, David guessed. But there had to be a way to make this work. He wasn't giving up on the boy without a fight. "Look, Ms. Morris, I appreciate your concerns. I know you want what's best for Jared. Why don't you let me come down and talk this over in person? Maybe we can figure something out to help Jared take advantage of Uplink without causing any further problems."

"I don't see how, Mr. Sloan." Her voice was weary—and resigned.

"Will you at least give me a few minutes of your time to talk this through?"

"I guess that couldn't hurt."

Consulting his watch, David did a rapid mental calculation. "I can be there in half an hour. Would that be okay?"

"Yes. That's fine. But I think you're wasting your time."

"I'm willing to take that chance."

"All right. I'll see you about noon."

As David ended the call, Caroline gave him a troubled look. As she'd watched his face and listened to his side of the exchange, she'd gotten the gist of the conversation. Something had happened to Jared. And he was dropping out. Questions sprang to her lips, but she waited while David gathered his thoughts and let him speak first.

"Jared had a run-in with his old gang last night. I got the impression they roughed him up. Enough to give his grandmother—and maybe him—cold feet. I'm assuming it was an intimidation tactic, to keep him from straying too far. They must have found out about Uplink. She says he's going to withdraw from the program."

"But you're going to talk to her?"

"Yes. I'm not sure what good it will do. Her mind seems to be made up. But I can't let him walk away from this without exploring every option first."

"I agree. Why don't I come with you? Maybe between us we can convince her to let him continue."

The offer surprised him, but before he could respond, Ella came up beside them. "Sounds like a good idea to me. Two heads are always better than one." She gave the room a quick scan, then directed her next comment to David. "I've gathered up all the extra material. Do you need me for anything else today?"

"No. Thanks for your help, Ella. I'll see you Monday."

"I'll be there. In the meantime, you work on that grandma. Together." She gave Caroline a wink. "And don't be shy, honey. You just speak right up to that lady. Go for the heartstrings. You'll be much better at that than David." With a wave, she went to retrieve her purse.

A smile touched the corners of David's lip. "I guess I have my orders."

"It seems I do, too," Caroline replied, amused.

"Let's give it a try, then. We can take my car. Since it's not the best part of town, we ought to stick close."

His suggestion made sense, so Caroline just nodded and reached for her purse.

Twenty minutes later, as they pulled up in front of the apartment building where Jared lived, David's lips settled into a grim line. Calling the dilapidated, five-story building with a dozen plastic-covered, broken windows and a small bare patch of earth in front a tenement would be too generous. A few youngsters were playing with a cardboard box in a side yard, and rap music blared from one of the open windows. In a vacant lot next door, a clump of wild tiger lilies had somehow managed to gain a foothold, providing the one touch of beauty in the desolate setting.

When David turned to Caroline, it was clear that the abject poverty and dismal environment had made a deep impression on her as well. Her face reflected sadness as she stared at the surroundings, and when he caught a glimmer in her eyes, he knew she was fighting back tears. All at once he was sorry he'd brought her. If he thought it was safe, he'd suggest she wait in the car and spare her a visit inside, which he suspected was as bad— or worse—than the outside. But there was no way he was leaving her alone in this neighborhood.

Reaching out, he laid a gentle hand on her shoulder. "This wasn't such a good idea. It's not very pretty down here."

His tender, caring touch choked her up even more, and she tried to swallow past the lump in her throat. "I've seen worse. I spent time in the Middle East, remember? But I'm always blown away when I come across poverty like this in our country. In a land where so many have so much, where a few miles from here people drive Mercedes and belong to country clubs and live in five-thousand-square-foot homes." She took another second to compose herself, then turned to him. "Ready?"

"Yes. I'll get your door."

She waited for him to come around, and he took her arm as they walked toward the entrance. A group of teenage boys sat on a stoop at the next building, and as he and Caroline picked their way over the cracked and buckled concrete sidewalk, whistles and catcalls followed their progress. David's grip on her elbow tightened in an instinctive, protective gesture. Once more, he regretted bringing her into this environment.

By unspoken mutual consent, they climbed the stairs instead of taking a dark, dingy elevator ride to the third floor. But the stairwell wasn't much better. The smell of stale urine assailed their nostrils, and garbage was wedged in every corner—except for the one where an older man slept with an empty whisky bottle beside him. More than ever, David resolved to do everything in his power to help Grace Morris find a way to feel comfortable—and safe—letting Jared participate in Uplink. It might be the boy's one and only chance to escape from this world.

When they reached the third floor, a long, dim, deserted corridor stretched before them, echoing with the noise coming from behind the dozens of closed doors. Shouts, curses, rap music, the blare of a TV set turned to full volume, a child crying—the cacophony of sound assaulted their ears. Resolving to get out of the hallway as fast as possible, David urged Caroline forward. She followed without protest, making it clear she was of the same mindset. Three doors down they came to Jared's apartment, and David knocked.

Within seconds, a woman's muffled voice came from the other side. "Who is it?"

"David Sloan."

A lock slid back, and an older woman cracked the door to peer out at them. Then she pulled it open and stepped aside, motioning them in. With a firm click she shut the door behind them and slid the lock back into place. "How do you do? I'm Grace Morris." She extended a gnarled, work-worn hand.

Both recognized her at once from Jared's photo. David took her hand first. "I'm David Sloan. This is Caroline James, from the *Chronicle,* who has agreed to be one of Jared's mentors at the newspaper. She was at today's meeting and offered to come with me."

Caroline took the woman's rough, sinewy hand as well—a hand that spoke of too much exposure to hard work and abrasive detergent. "It's nice to meet you, Ms. Morris."

The woman gestured toward a couch and rocking chair in the tiny living room. "Please sit down. May I offer you something to drink?"

Glancing at Caroline, David shook his head. "No, thanks. We're fine."

As she and David took a seat on the couch, Caroline gave the room a discreet perusal. Though the furnishings were shabby and the ceiling bore water stains, the apartment was tidy and spotless. A hand-crocheted afghan draped over the couch camouflaged the thread-bare patches in the fabric, and a bud vase containing one of the lilies from the vacant lot next door sat on a small table beside a worn Bible. Photos of Jared at various ages were grouped in cheap frames on a small credenza, and pictures of scenic vistas—the kind found on many calendars—brightened the walls.

As Grace Morris sat in the rocking chair at a right angle to the window, the sunlight threw the lines in her face into sharp relief. She looked like a woman who had had a hard life, one filled with care and worry. Yet her demeanor and bearing conveyed dignity and strength. As if she'd found a way to deal with the unfair hand life had dealt her without growing bitter. Caroline's gaze flickered to the Bible, and she suspected that book was the sustaining force in the woman's life. Jared's photo had suggested as much.

"Thank you for seeing us, Ms. Morris," David began. "I hope you don't mind that I brought Caroline along, but she's taken a great interest in Jared as well."

"I appreciate that very much."

"Is he here?"

She glanced toward the bedroom. "He's been sleeping. I didn't want to wake him."

"Can you tell us what happened last night?" David prodded gently.

A shadow passed over the woman's face. "He went out to pick up some medicine for me at the pharmacy. On the way back, some of the members of his gang jumped him. He's been trying to break off with them." Pausing, she reached over and laid her hand on the Bible. "I've been praying for that for a long time. Those boys are bad news. And they don't like defectors. They were putting pressure on Jared to get more involved, and when they heard about Uplink, they figured he was slipping away for good. Last night was a strong message that he better come back into the fold." She removed her glasses, closing her eyes as she massaged the bridge of her nose. Then she replaced the glasses and looked at David and Caroline. "I want Jared to find a way out of here. I want something better than this for my boy. But I also want him to have a long life. And I'm afraid if he continues with Uplink, that might not happen."

His face intent, David leaned forward. "How badly hurt is he, Ms. Morris?"

"Enough that we spent twelve hours in the emergency room. At first he didn't want to go. He knew there'd be questions. But he was having trouble breathing, which scared him—and me, too. By eleven last night I convinced him that we needed to get help."

"What did the doctors—"

A door opened down the hallway off the living room, and David stopped speaking. The sound of shuffling feet followed. Neither he nor Caroline had a view of the hall from where they sat, but it was in Grace's line of sight. She rose just as Jared appeared in the doorway, leaning against the wall and clutching his side.

"Nan, the bandage on my arm came off. Do we have any…"

Caroline shifted in her seat, and the movement

caught Jared's attention. Startled, he jerked his head their way and stared at her, then at David. "What's going on?" He directed the question to his grandmother.

"Mr. Sloan called to see why you missed the Uplink meeting, and asked if he could visit to talk with me. Ms. James came along."

As the two conversed, David took a quick inventory of Jared. It was clear from his bent posture that the boy was in pain from injuries David couldn't see. But there were plenty of visible injuries as well. Jared's right eye was almost swollen shut, his lip was puffy and split, and on his upper arm, just below the sleeve of his T-shirt, there was a jagged line of stitches.

A quick glance in Caroline's direction told him that she was just as shocked as he by the boy's condition.

Jared tried to straighten up, but the effort was too much and he winced. "Didn't you tell them I'm dropping out?"

"Yes."

"We'd like to find a way for you to stay in the program, Jared," David said.

The boy looked at him, his face bleak. "It ain't gonna happen, man. I won't put Nan through the worry."

"But there has to be a way," Caroline countered. Now that she'd seen his living conditions, she was more determined than ever to help him find a way out. She didn't want the gang's intimidation tactics to rob Jared of the best opportunity he might ever have to escape this environment.

"I already have two broken ribs. I'm not angling for two more. Or worse."

"Look, why don't you sit down for a minute while we discuss this?" David rose and moved toward the boy, whose instinctive reaction was to recoil. Slowing his advance, David stopped short of Jared and reached out a hand. "Just lean on me, okay? There's nothing wrong with admitting you need some help. We all do at times."

For several seconds Jared stared at David. Then his shoulders slumped. "Okay. Thanks," he mumbled.

David moved closer, and the tall, lanky teenager grasped his arm as he shuffled toward the couch. Caroline moved over to make room for them both, and David eased the boy down before taking his own seat.

"Okay. Let's think about this a little. It's obvious that we need to get you out of this environment. Ms. Morris, is there anywhere else Jared could live for the summer? A relative who might take him in, in a different part of town? Somewhere away from the gang, a place where they might be less likely to bother him?"

"I have one sister. A widow. She lives in Webster Groves, but we haven't spoken in a long time."

"Webster is close to the *Chronicle*. And far enough away from North St. Louis that the gang might leave Jared alone." It sounded like the perfect arrangement to David.

"I've always taken care of Jared by myself. No one's ever offered to help, and I've never asked. I don't plan to start now," Grace replied. "Besides, like I said, my sister and I haven't spoken for years."

A family rift. David could relate to that. He knew he was treading on sensitive ground, stepping onto a potential minefield, by pursuing this. But he had to take the chance, for Jared's sake.

"Ms. Morris, I admire the fact that you've always cared for Jared on your own. You deserve a lot of credit for that. But maybe the best way you can take care of him right now is to ask your sister for help. I understand why that may not be easy. I had a rift with my own brother, and I've always regretted the fact that we didn't resolve it before he died." His voice grew hoarse on the last word, and he cleared his throat. "There's still time for you, though. And in the process, you'll be doing your best to take care of Jared, just as you always have."

Grace considered that for a moment. Then she reached for the Bible on the table beside her and cradled it in her hands. "I tried to contact her once, to mend our fences, when her husband died three years ago. But she didn't want any part of a reconciliation. I doubt she's changed her mind since then."

"And there's no one else?"

"No."

Stymied, David leaned forward and clasped his hands between his knees. He couldn't dismiss Grace's worry. Leaving Jared in this environment while he participated in Uplink was asking for trouble. But there seemed to be no other option. Unless…unless Jared lived with him for the summer. It wasn't ideal, of course. The board had warned him early on not to get personally involved with individual students. Too many of them had stories of hardship, and the emotional toll could be great. As a result, the board preferred that the executive director be compassionate but maintain a professional distance. Yet if David didn't step over that line, Jared would be out. And he couldn't let that happen.

"Look, Ms. Morris, this isn't something in my job description. But I care about what happens to Jared. If there's no other option, he would be welcome to stay with me over the summer."

All three people in the room stared at him. Jared looked shocked. Ms. Morris seemed taken aback, but touched. Caroline looked… He didn't want to dwell on the soft warmth in her eyes. So he turned back to Jared's grandmother and focused on her.

"I don't know what to say, Mr. Sloan," she told him.

"I hope you'll say yes."

Something flickered to life in Jared's eyes. Something that looked a lot like hope rekindling. He turned to his grandmother. "I'd like to be part of Uplink, Nan."

Indecision registered on her face. She looked down again at the Bible in her lap, then shook her head. "That's a very kind offer, Mr. Sloan. But it's too much of an imposition."

For most of the visit, Caroline had remained silent. But she could feel the tension in the boy beside her, knew at some instinctive level that even though he might not be very good with the spoken word, he wanted this opportunity. Very much. Yet he would defer to his grandmother's wishes. At the same time, she understood the woman's reluctance to accept David's generous offer. It *was* a tremendous imposition. That left only one other option.

Leaning forward, Caroline spoke to the older woman, her voice earnest and empathetic. "Would you consider contacting your sister again, for Jared's sake, Ms. Morris? I know you said you tried three years ago, but many things can change in three years…or three months…or even overnight." The shadow of pain that darkened her face wasn't lost on David, and he had to stifle an urge to reach over and give her hand an encouraging squeeze. Instead, he linked his clasped hands more tightly. "Maybe it would be worth trying to contact her one more time. You wouldn't have anything to lose, and perhaps you'd have a lot to gain."

Jared's grandmother looked at the three people sitting across from her on the sofa, waiting for her decision. If two strangers were willing to go out of their way to give her boy the chance she'd always prayed for, how could she refuse their appeal to make one more attempt to contact Dara? Maybe her sister would rebuff her again. But maybe, just maybe, she'd listen this time. And with God's help, they might even be able to recapture the closeness they'd once shared. Its absence had been a great sorrow in Grace's life. Perhaps the woman from the *Chronicle* was right, and Dara's attitude had changed. But even if it hadn't, she couldn't argue with Caroline James's other comment. She didn't have anything to lose by trying.

With sudden resolve, Grace clutched her Bible to her chest and took a deep breath. "All right. I'll give my sister a call."

As she voiced her decision, the looks of elation on the three faces across from her were almost enough reward in themselves.

Chapter Eight

"That was a very generous offer you made to Jared."

As David merged into the traffic on the highway and headed west, he risked a quick glance at Caroline. "I want him to succeed. That seemed like the only way to make it happen."

"Most people wouldn't make such a personal investment."

A rueful look settled over his face. "Nor does the board encourage it. This whole business with Jared has been risky from day one."

"Yet you're willing to take a chance on him."

"Yeah. And for a guy who's been risk-averse most of his life, it's a bit unsettling. But I think Jared has a lot to offer, and I'd hate to see his talent go to waste. I assume that's why you're taking a chance on him, too."

When she didn't respond, David sent her an inquisitive look. She was staring out the front window, her face troubled. "What's wrong?"

At his comment, she turned toward him. "I wish my motivations were that selfless. He is a very gifted writer and photographer, and I'd like to help him find his calling. But I also keep thinking about Michael, how a mentor helped him get his act together and develop his talent. And how Michael always wanted to pay back that kindness by doing the same for another young person. I guess, in a way, I feel like I need to do this for Michael, as a final tribute. And as an atonement for the part I played in his death."

Her voice choked on the last word, and without stopping to think, David removed one hand from the wheel and reached over to touch her cheek. She turned to him in surprise, and he found his hand cupping her chin, her skin smooth and silky against his fingers.

Clearing his throat, he retrieved his hand and transferred it to the wheel, curling his fingers around it in a tight, steadying grip. "I feel the same way," he admitted, his voice a bit rough around the edges. "I guess neither of us has purely altruistic motives."

After that unexpected touch, it took her a second to refocus. "I—I suppose the important thing is that good may come out of it. And I think Michael would be pleased, don't you?"

"Yeah, I do. Jared's exactly the kind of kid he would have chosen to help if he'd had the opportunity."

"Do you think his grandmother will have any luck with her sister?"

"Hard to say, since we don't know what prompted the falling-out." He consulted his watch. "Listen, I don't know about you, but I'm starving. I just grabbed a doughnut this morning at the meeting. Can I interest you in some lunch?"

The man was full of surprises today, Caroline thought, taken aback by the suggestion. She turned to him, noting the strong chin, the firm lips, the well-shaped nose revealed in profile. Sometimes it was hard to believe that he and Michael were brothers. There was little physical resemblance. And their personalities were just as different. Michael had crackled with energy, infusing those he met with excitement and enthusiasm. David was more steady, more solid, instilling trust and confidence in everyone around him. Michael had lived on the edge, carrying a whiff of danger with him; David resided on a firm foundation, and he made people feel safe and protected.

After their first meeting weeks before, Caroline had vowed to cut all ties to David. Being with him had dredged up unhappy memories and resentments. But as their paths had begun to cross—and would continue to cross throughout the summer if Jared ended up participating in Uplink—she'd come to see his warm, compassionate, caring side. And as she'd witnessed his deep faith and integrity, she'd found herself not just enduring his company, as she'd expected, but enjoying it.

So the idea of sharing lunch with him held a certain appeal. Besides, it might also give her a chance to ask a few questions about the rift between the two brothers, as her mother has suggested. Already her perspective on that had shifted, and she had a feeling that if she heard David's side of the story it might shift even more. For reasons she didn't quite understand, she was beginning to hope it would.

When the silence between them lengthened, David flicked her an amused glance. "If it's taking you that long to decide, you must not be as hungry as I am."

With a start, she forced her thoughts back to the present. And made her decision. "As a matter of fact, I am. Lunch would be nice. Thanks."

For a brief instant, David seemed as surprised by her acceptance as she'd been by the invitation, but he recovered quickly. "Great. Any suggestions on a place? I'm too new in town to know the good spots yet."

"How about Café Provençal, in Kirkwood? They have a great patio and the weather is perfect today for outdoor dining."

"Sounds good. But you'll have to direct me."

She did so, and once seated at a wrought-iron table under the large awning, he nodded his approval. "I like this. Do you come here often?"

"No. I've been here for dinner a few times. But it's more of a special-occasion place at night. During the day, it's pretty casual."

"I don't know. I think a special-occasion place is defined more by the company than the ambiance."

His tone was conversational, but something in his eyes sent an odd tingle up her spine. Caroline was saved from having to respond by the appearance of the waitress, who recited the list of specials. As she departed, a man about David's age, dressed in khakis and a golf shirt, rose from a nearby table and walked over to them.

"David? I thought that was you."

At the greeting, David turned in surprise. Then he

smiled and rose, extending his hand. "Chuck Williams! What are you doing here?"

"I'm on vacation, visiting my wife's family." He gestured toward a table in the corner, where an attractive woman was seated with an older couple.

"Chuck, this is Caroline James. Caroline, Chuck was an associate of mine at my old firm in Chicago until he switched companies about a year ago."

After they exchanged a few pleasantries, Chuck turned his attention back to David. "So what are you doing in St. Louis?"

"I took a job here with a nonprofit organization almost six months ago."

"No kidding? When you turned down that fabulous offer in New York right before I left because you didn't want to disrupt your mom's life by moving her again, I figured you'd be in Chicago forever. How is she?"

"She passed away a year ago. Not long after you left."

Sympathy suffused the man's face. "I'm so sorry, David. That had to be tough. I know how much she meant to you. And what great care you gave her."

"Thanks. It's been hard. But I have a new life now, doing something I love. It seems all things work toward God's plan."

"Well, I'm happy for you, then." He turned back to Caroline. "It was nice to meet you. And good luck with the new job," he told David.

"Thanks."

As the man returned to his table and David took his seat again, Caroline reached for her water glass, trying to buy herself a few seconds to digest the information she'd just heard. David had turned down a major promotion in order to remain in Chicago because he had felt it was in his mother's best interest. It was yet another piece of information confirming that David hadn't been selfish in his decision to put their mother in a nursing facility, as Michael had thought.

"You look a bit pensive."

At David's comment, Caroline tried for a smile. "I was just thinking about Michael." That was true. Sort of. And it might give her an indirect avenue to ask the questions that were on her mind.

"Anything in particular?"

"About his passion for life. And his spontaneity. And how much he cared for the people he loved."

"Yeah. I agree. I always admired him for his loyalty and his willingness to embrace life without agonizing over every little decision. I had a case of hero worship for him ever since I was a little kid. He always seemed larger than life, somehow. I tried to emulate him, but we were just too different. He was athletic, I was academic. He was the daredevil type, always looking for adventure, while I was the cautious one. Even though I sometimes cringed at his recklessness, I couldn't help but admire his fearlessness." A smile touched his lips, and the firm planes of his face softened in recollection. "I remember one time, when he was about ten or eleven, he was convinced that he could jump from the roof of our garage to the roof of the toolshed next door. So he put on his superhero cape and climbed up on the roof—a feat which, in and of itself, seemed incredibly brave to me at the time. Then he proceeded to attempt the jump."

"What happened?"

"We all took a trip to the emergency room while he got a dozen stitches in his chin." David chuckled and shook his head. "The whole incident seemed to bother us a lot more than it bothered him. By the next day, he was ready to try it again. And he would have, too, if my dad hadn't threatened to pull him out of soccer if he did."

That sounded like Michael, Caroline reflected, her own lips turning up into a wistful smile. "Well, you may have had a case of hero worship, but Michael also had great admiration and respect for you. He was always bragging about his little brother."

That was news to David. Michael had never been the type to give voice to those kinds of thoughts. At least not to him. The love between them had been strong, but not often verbalized. "Thanks for telling me that. It means a lot. And that's another way that Michael reminds me of Jared. Verbal communication wasn't his strong suit."

Caroline gave David a surprised look. "I thought he was very good with words."

"Maybe he was with you. At least, I hope he was. An engaged woman has a right to hear what's in the heart of the man she loves. But with most people, Michael kept his feelings to himself. He might have been willing to take chances physically, like the day he jumped off the garage roof, but he was a lot more cautious about sharing what was in his heart. That's why it was difficult to talk to him about the situation with Mom."

A perfect opening, Caroline thought. But she needed to proceed with caution. "He was very upset about that," she ventured.

"I know. We both let anger get in the way of communication. I'm sorry we never resolved our differences. I'll regret that until the day I die."

With the tip of her finger, Caroline traced the trail of a drop of condensation down her glass, thinking how much it looked like a tear. When she spoke, her voice was soft and tinged with melancholy. "I have to admit that I resented you for a long time after Michael died. I felt that your argument with him was on his mind that day in the marketplace, that maybe it distracted him and made him less alert than usual. That if he'd been focused on the situation, he might have noticed something awry and stayed out of harm's way. The fact is, though, suicide bombers don't often tip their hands."

"Maybe not. But I've always felt guilty about it, anyway. Still, I don't know what I'd do differently. When you visited at Christmas, Mom had a couple of good days. But right after that, she went downhill so fast that even I had a hard time believing it. And it had to be much more difficult for Michael to grasp the extent and swiftness of her decline from thousands of miles away. Within weeks, I was afraid to leave her alone for even a few minutes. Once, on a Saturday, I left her in the kitchen for less than three minutes and came back to find that she'd turned on all the burners on the stove and put empty pots on each one. Another time, I took her to church and when I stopped to talk with a friend, she disappeared. Ten frantic minutes later I found her wandering down the middle of the street."

Taking a deep breath, David raked his fingers through his hair. "To make matters worse, I was having a harder and harder time finding reliable help during the day. Since night help was even more difficult to arrange, I started sleeping at her house. I cut down on my business trips as much as I could, because it was almost impossible to find anyone to stay with her for extended periods. I know Michael wanted me to wait until you came home for the wedding before taking any action, but there was no way I could do that. I didn't want to break our promise to Mom any more than he did, but for her own sake, she needed round-the-clock supervision. There just wasn't any other option. Michael wouldn't—or couldn't—accept that. And, to be honest, I resented him for abdicating his responsibility in dealing with the issue. He left it all to me, then got angry when I addressed the problem. It was a bad situation all around."

As Caroline listened to David's explanation, her heart began to ache for him. Until now, she'd never realized the weight of the burden he'd carried. It also became clear to her that despite Michael's angry assessment, David's decision hadn't been arbitrary. It had been born out of necessity. Distance had insulated Michael from the harsh reality of their mother's condition. And perhaps he simply hadn't wanted to acknowledge it, as David had implied. It was hard to come to grips with breaking a promise to someone you loved, even if it was in their best interest. Yet David had had the courage to do that, to handle the heart-wrenching situation alone in a way that reflected deep love and great integrity. Earlier in the day she'd admired his generosity for the offer he'd made to Jared's grandmother. Now her admiration grew yet again. Respect and esteem for this special man filled her heart, easing out any lingering resentment.

The waitress delivered their food then, and Caroline searched for an appropriate response to David's story. She settled for something simple. Reaching over, she laid her hand on his. "Thank you for sharing that with me, David. It gives me a different perspective on the whole situation."

Startled by her touch, David looked at her—and his lungs stopped working. In her hazel eyes he saw kindness and caring and empathy—and no trace of the wariness or resentment that had lurked in their depths until today. For the first time she was seeing him as a unique person—not as a future brother-in-law, not as an enemy, not as a business associate. But as David Sloan, the man. The individual. And it just about did him in.

Swallowing, he dropped his gaze to her slender fingers, delicate and pale against his sun-browned hand. And a sudden yearning swept over him—a yearning to touch her, to hold her, to let her warmth fill his life and chase away the loneliness that had plagued him for the past couple of years, when his first sight of her had awakened a hunger in him for all the things he'd been missing by putting love on the back burner.

As she removed her hand and turned her attention to her lunch, David forced himself to do the same. But he knew that the hunger inside him, the empty place in his heart, could never be satisfied by the chicken salad sandwich on his plate.

* * *

Grace Morris reached for the phone, then let her hand drop back to her lap. She'd had to do a lot of hard things in her life. Bury her husband. Watch her one child, her beloved daughter, die of a drug overdose. Do menial, physical work that left her bone-weary. Raise her grandson alone. But calling Dara ranked right up near the top.

Reaching for her Bible, as she had during many of the hard times, Grace opened it to Matthew, to the passage that had given her comfort and sustained her in her darkest days. Once more she read the familiar words. "Come to me, all you who labor and are burdened, and I will give you rest. Take my yoke upon you, and learn from me, for I am meek and humble of heart—and you will find rest for your souls."

Closing her eyes, Grace added her own prayer. *Lord, please help Dara find it in her heart to understand. Please help her to see the truth, to know that I love her and would never do anything to hurt her. Help us to be sisters again. But even if that can't be, please fill her heart with compassion for Jared so that he can have a better life. Amen.*

Once more, Grace reached for the phone. This time she tapped in the number. Though her hand was trembling, she felt steadier inside, her courage bolstered by her prayer. When her sister answered on the third ring, she forced the words past her tight throat.

"Dara? It's Grace." Holding her breath, Grace waited for a response, praying that it wouldn't be just a hangup. *Please, Lord, at least let her talk to me.*

Several seconds of shocked silence passed. But at last the other woman spoke in a cautious voice. "Hello, Grace."

"Thank you for not hanging up on me."

"I've gotten past that, I guess."

That was a good start, Grace thought. "It's been a long time since we talked."

"Yes. It has."

"I'm sorry for all the misunderstanding between us. I've missed having a sister."

After a few seconds, Dara responded. "I have, too." Her quiet admission surprised Grace. As did her next comment. "I even thought about calling you once or twice. But I could never bring myself to do it. The fact is, I should never have gotten angry at you. It was just easier, somehow, to blame you than to accept the fact that George was…that he wasn't the most faithful husband."

Grace thought back to that Christmas when George had cornered her in the kitchen after having one too many drinks. Recalled how he'd backed her against the refrigerator and kissed her, suggesting that he'd be happy to ease her loneliness now that she was a widow. Grace had heard rumors for years that George had a tendency to stray, but she'd never believed them. Never wanted to believe them. Then Dara had come into the kitchen at the worst possible moment. She'd stormed over, yanked George away and lit into Grace about seducing her own brother-in-law when he was half-drunk. She'd said a lot of bad things that had hurt Grace and incited her own anger. How could the sister she'd loved all her life make such terrible accusations?

That had been nine years ago, right before Jared had

come to live with her. Though Grace had made an overture to mend their fences when George died, her sister had rebuffed it. She and Dara hadn't talked since.

"I never encouraged him, Dara."

"I know that now. All the stories I heard after he died confirmed what I'd suspected for years, but refused to accept. Ever since then, I've wanted to call you. But pride got in my way. I didn't want to admit that I couldn't even keep my own husband interested."

"The problem wasn't in you, Dara."

"Sometimes I wonder about that. But it's over now, anyway. And more and more I realize how much I miss having you in my life. I was just afraid it was too late. I said some awful things to you."

"I was angry about that for a long time," Grace admitted. "But I prayed a lot about it through the years, and I finally let the anger go. I've been wanting to call you for a long time, but I was afraid you'd cut me off."

"Fear and pride. Two destructive emotions. We're quite a pair, I guess. What's that saying about an old fool? But at least you tried to reconnect when George died. Considering how I treated you then, I'm surprised you tried again. I figured the next attempt would have to come from me."

Now came the moment of truth. And Grace figured honesty was the best way to handle it. "I guess maybe that would have been the case if I wasn't worried about Jared."

"Is there something wrong with him?"

Plunging into the story, Grace gave Dara the highlights, then summed up the impetus for her call. "So unless I can find a place for him to stay for the summer where he'll be away from the gang, he's going to have to turn down the opportunity. I just don't want to risk losing him. But I do want him to have a better life. I guess my love for him helped me overcome my fear about calling. I need your help, Dara. If you can find it in your heart to give him a room for ten weeks, it could make all the difference in the world to him."

When her request was met with silence, Grace fought down the panic that welled up inside her. "I know this is coming at you out of the blue, Dara. I don't expect an answer right away. You can call me back after you think about it. And if you don't want to take this on, I'll understand. I realize what an imposition it would be."

"You did take me by surprise, Grace."

"I'm sure I did. Like I said, I'd just be grateful if you'd consider it. For Jared's sake, not mine."

"Is he a good boy?"

"He's good at heart. That's why he's trying to break his gang ties and make something better of his life. He's honest, and if he makes a promise, he keeps it. But I won't lie to you. He's had some rough stretches. His grades aren't the best, and I've had a tough time keeping him in school. That's why Uplink is such a godsend. I've been praying for the past two years that something will help him turn his life around, and I think this is it."

"I'm not sure I know how to deal with a teenager, Grace. Since George and I never had children, I don't have any experience with young people."

"Jared is very self-sufficient. All he really needs is a place to sleep. I'll be happy to contribute toward his meals and any other expenses he might incur."

"Are you still working?"

"Yes."

"Doing what?"

"The same thing I've always done."

Dara shifted the phone on her ear. George might not have been faithful, but he'd at least given her a comfortable life and left her well-fixed. She could afford to take the boy on for the summer. And with two empty bedrooms, she had plenty of room. "I'd like to meet the boy, at least," she said.

Grace said a silent prayer of thanks before she responded. "He'd like to meet you, too."

"Why don't you bring him out on Saturday?"

"You want me to come, too?"

"Of course. I don't remember Jared very well. It will be less awkward if you're there. Besides, we have a lot to catch up on."

"I doubt we can make much headway in one meeting."

"I'm hoping it's the first of many."

A cleansing wave of happiness swept over Grace, washing away the debris of their broken relationship and leaving a smooth, fresh expanse in its wake.

"We'll be there, Dara."

"Make it about eleven, if that's okay. And plan to stay for lunch."

"All right. And thank you."

"Thank *you*. For having the courage to take the first step. I'll see you Saturday."

As Grace replaced the phone, she reached over once more to pick up her Bible, her heart overflowing with gratitude. And as she placed it against her heart, she smiled.

God was good.

Chapter Nine

"Take a look at these."

Ignoring her half-shut door, Bill Baker strolled into Caroline's office without knocking and dropped several black-and-white photos on her desk.

If he wasn't such a great photographer—and if he didn't have a heart of gold—Caroline wondered if she'd be willing to put up with Bill's brusque style. As it was, she just set aside the layouts for the next week's edition and reached for the photos, her mind still on the changes she needed to call into the production department.

But her focus shifted abruptly as the photos caught her attention. The subject of each was a child with some sort of disability. One little boy was laughing in delight as he was lifted from his wheelchair to the back of a horse. A young blind girl was engrossed in shaping a vase on a potter's wheel, her face alight with wonder as her hands molded the clay. The joyful expression of a boy with Down syndrome had been caught at the perfect instant, as he reeled in a fish. Each of the remaining photos was just as compelling, capturing expressions and moments that spoke of joy and hope in the midst of problem-plagued lives.

When she finished, she looked up at Bill. "Let me guess. Jared."

"That's right." He propped a hip on the corner of Caroline's desk. "I sent him to cover a day camp for disabled children. It was his first solo assignment. My only instruction was to capture the spirit of the event, and this is what he came back with."

Leaning back in her chair, Caroline steepled her fingers. "Amazing."

"That's the word for it. I figured you'd want to see these before I turn them in to production."

"You were right. Thanks. How's everything been going in general?" Three weeks into the internship, Jared seemed to have settled in. There'd been a few rough patches at first as he adjusted to his new living arrangement and the eight-to-five working world, but nothing that had caused Caroline any great concern.

"Better and better. The attitude problem is disappearing, and he's done a good job at all the shoots he's been on with me. He remembers every critique I make of his work, and incorporates my suggestions into the next assignment. That's why I figured he was ready to go solo for the camp story."

"You figured right."

"How's he faring from the writing end?"

"Also improving. He doesn't take as much offense

when I offer constructive criticism. And we're going to run a bylined piece in the next edition."

"He'll like that." Bill rose, gathered up the photos and headed toward the door, glancing across the newsroom through Caroline's glass-walled office toward Jared's cubicle. The boy was concentrating at his computer and oblivious to their perusal. "I need to catch him before he takes off. I'll talk to you later."

As Bill strode toward Jared, Caroline assessed the changes in their intern. He'd appeared the first day in jeans, new loafers and a golf shirt—a great improvement over the baggy pants and ripped shirts that seemed to be his typical attire. After two weeks, the dreadlocks had been sheared into a clean-cut, close-cropped style. Although the employees had been welcoming, he'd kept to himself at first, standing apart in the break room when other staffers gathered to chat over coffee, and rebuffing lunch invitations. But in the past couple of days, she'd noticed him leaving at lunchtime with two of the younger employees who frequented a local sandwich shop. She'd seen that as a good sign, an indication that he was adjusting and beginning to feel comfortable.

If Caroline's relief at the smooth transition was considerable, she knew David's was even greater. He'd put his career on the line by taking a chance on Jared. A chance that seemed to be paying off. She and David spoke on a regular basis, and he'd stopped by a couple of times to visit Jared on the job site, as he did with all of the interns. For reasons she didn't want to examine too closely, she found herself looking forward to those visits. Much more than was prudent. When Jared's internship ended, there would be little reason for David to stay in touch. Considering her antipathy toward the man just a few weeks before, she should be happy about that. Instead, she felt melancholy, which in turn made her feel uncomfortable. Again, for reasons she wasn't inclined to scrutinize.

To distract herself, Caroline turned toward her credenza and opened the top drawer. Withdrawing the envelope she'd placed there last week, she scanned the announcement from the national journalism association about a competition for high school students. Winners would attend a two-week intensive program in New York conducted by major names in the fields of journalism and photography. The entry required at least one letter of recommendation from a member of the professional organization, as well as a feature story written and photographed by the entrant. When Caroline had seen it, she'd thought of Jared at once. With some judicious coaching, she'd pit his work not just against other students, but against many pros she'd met. Since the deadline wasn't for six weeks, she'd been biding her time, waiting to see how things worked out with the internship. But at this point, she saw no reason to delay suggesting that he enter.

Just then Jared rose, and Bill laid a hand on his shoulder. Where once he would have flinched, now she saw a quick grin flash across the boy's face. Another positive sign, she thought. As she headed for her door to discuss the competition with him, he reached for his backpack under the desk. Checking her watch, she noted that it was already after five—and he had a bus to catch.

His great-aunt's home wasn't far, but the bus schedule in the county was somewhat limited, and if he missed his ride it would be a long walk. Deciding that their discussion could wait until first thing the next morning, Caroline put the competition materials aside and went back to work.

Almost three hours passed before quitting time came for her. The day before the paper went to press was always grueling. Then again, she hadn't gotten into journalism for its regular hours, she thought, a wry grin tugging at her lips as she reached for her tote. Hoisting it on her shoulder, she was just about to switch off the light in her office when her phone rang.

The temptation to ignore it was strong. She wasn't anxious to extend her already long day. Nevertheless, she circled back around her desk to check her caller ID, hesitating at the unfamiliar number. What if it was a hot lead for a great story? Her journalistic training kicked in, and ignoring the hunger pangs that told her it was well past dinnertime, she reached for the phone.

"Caroline James."

"Caroline, it's David. I tried your home number, but when I didn't get an answer I took a chance you might still be at the office."

The sound of his voice brought a smile to her lips. "Mondays are always late nights for me because we go to press on Tuesday. I was just heading out."

"Well, I don't want to delay you. I was just in the neighborhood and thought I'd drop off the midterm evaluation form instead of mailing it. We always ask our mentors to give us a brief written progress report on their intern halfway through the program. Is there a night slot I could leave it in?"

"How far away are you?"

"About five minutes."

"I'll just wait for you in the lobby."

"Are you sure you don't mind?"

"No. I could use a couple of minutes to sit and veg."

"Okay. I'll be there soon."

As it turned out, David didn't arrive for almost fifteen minutes. When she finally saw him striding down the sidewalk, his suit-and-tie attire suggested that he, too, had had a long workday. She met him at the door before he could even press the buzzer.

"Sorry for the delay," he apologized. "I got stopped by a train a few blocks up on Kirkwood Road."

Smiling, she reached for the envelope he held out to her and slid it into her shoulder tote. "It happens all the time. There's a route over the tracks, but only the locals know about it. I'll give you directions sometime."

"Thanks."

When he hesitated, Caroline searched his face. He looked tired, she thought. As if he'd not only been putting in long hours, but perhaps investing too much of himself in his job—worrying about the students, worrying about making the program a success, worrying about fulfilling the plan he seemed to feel that God had for him. That was another difference between the two brothers, she mused. Michael hadn't been a worrier. Or much of a planner. He'd always lived for the moment, choosing to let tomorrow take care of itself. A worrier herself, Caroline had found that quality appealing—

and liberating. But while she'd agreed with Michael that worry taken to extremes was counterproductive and could rob you of today, in retrospect she realized that he may have erred too much in the other direction. Worry in moderation could be constructive, allowing you to avoid mistakes. It could also foster compassion. The trick was finding the balance.

Caroline suspected that David hadn't done that yet. That he still took on the cares of those entrusted to him as if they were his own. Including every student in the Uplink program. And one student in particular. His next question confirmed her suspicion.

"How's Jared doing?"

"Great. Bill showed me some photos today that Jared took on his first solo assignment, a day camp for disabled children. They were fabulous. Every one displayed the signature quality we noticed in the work in his portfolio. And we're going to run a bylined story in the next edition. His writing was good to begin with, but it's gotten even better."

The subtle relaxing of David's features told her he welcomed that news even before he spoke. "I'm glad to hear it." He glanced over her shoulder, to the darkened offices. "Are you the last one here?"

"The managing editor is always the last to leave. At least on pre-press days. It goes with the territory."

"Can I walk you to your car?"

Surprised, she shook her head. "Thanks, but that's not necessary. There's a lot right behind the building. I'm just going to set the night alarm and pull the front door shut behind me, then head down the alley." She punched some numbers into the keypad beside the door, then stepped outside.

As she twisted the handle of the door to confirm that it had locked, David gave the narrow, dim passage a quick look. "I'd feel better about it if you'd let me see you to your car. My mother always told me that a gentleman should never let a lady walk down a dark alley alone." His lips quirked into a grin.

David was a gentleman, no question about that, Caroline reflected as she hoisted her shoulder tote higher. Even her mother would approve of his good manners. Not that it mattered, of course. It wasn't as if they were dating or anything.

But I wish we were.

The wistful but startling thought came to her unbidden. How in the world could she even think such a thing? This was the brother of the man she'd loved. The man she *still* loved. She wasn't interested in getting involved with *any* man, let alone this man. It just felt…wrong.

As David waited for Caroline's response, he wasn't quite sure what to make of the expressions flitting across her face. But he hoped she wasn't insulted. In today's politically correct world, it was sometimes hard to know just how chivalrous to be with women. "I know the offer is a bit old-fashioned, and to someone who's spent time in the Middle East it may seem like overkill. I hope I didn't offend you."

With an effort, Caroline reined in her wayward thoughts and tamped down the sudden staccato beat of her heart. "No. Not at all. I guess I've just gotten so used to taking care of myself that the offer surprised me. Thank you." Without waiting for him to respond, she headed for the alley.

He followed close behind her, since the passage wasn't wide enough to accommodate them side by side. Most of the time Caroline exited out the back door, right into the parking lot. She'd only used this route once or twice. And never in the evening. Even though it stayed light quite late this time of year, dusk had settled, and the deep shadows between the buildings were a bit unnerving. Despite the fact that she considered Kirkwood safe, and that she'd been alone in far more dangerous situations on assignments, she found David's presence comforting. It made her feel protected. While his offer might have been prompted by mere courtesy, it nevertheless made her feel cared for. And special, somehow.

When they emerged into the dimly lit parking area, he moved into step beside her. She gestured toward her car, which was wedged into a far corner of the lot. "I had to run an errand at lunch, and when I got back that was the only spot left. Most of the time I park much closer to the door." She stopped and turned to him. "Thanks again."

"I'm beginning to think you're trying to get rid of me."

"No, of course not." Her protest came fast. Too fast. The line from Shakespeare flashed through her mind, and a flush crept up her neck.

"Then I'll finish the job." His hand moved to the small of her back and he urged her forward with a firm, sure touch.

At his prompt, Caroline moved toward her car, deciding that silence was her best response. She had no idea what was going on with her equilibrium, but all at once she felt off balance and ill at ease. Later, when she was alone, she'd think this through. Right now, she just needed to get into the car and away from the man beside her, who seemed to be the cause of her problem.

Trying not to run, she picked up her pace. As she approached the car, she fumbled in her shoulder tote for her keys. "Are you just heading home from the office, too?"

When her question produced no response, Caroline sent David a questioning look. He was staring at the passenger door of her car with an odd expression, and when she turned in search of the cause, it hit her like a slap in the face.

Scratched into the maroon paint was a warning—"Back off"—followed by a single, crude term directed at her. She gasped at the vulgar reference.

David's hand tightened on her waist, and she turned to him. His mouth was set in a grim line, and all levity had vanished from his face. When he looked down at her, she saw worry in the depths of his brown eyes. "Do you have any idea what that might be about, besides the obvious?"

Although his tone was quiet and controlled, she could sense the tension in his body. The "obvious" was Jared, of course. But she didn't want to believe that.

"Maybe it's not what you assume."

"Can you think of any other explanation?"

In truth, she couldn't. She'd taken flak for stories in the past, but there was no issue hot enough right now to raise anyone's ire to a level that would push them to take this kind of action. "No."

"That's what I figured." David reached into his pocket and withdrew his cell phone.

"What are you doing?"

"Calling the police."

"I doubt it will do any good. The lot's deserted. This could have been done hours ago."

"It still needs to be reported. For insurance purposes, if nothing else."

She put out a hand to restrain him. "Look, David, I don't want to cause trouble for you or Jared. If this gets back to the Uplink board members, they'll give you a lot of grief. And it could jeopardize their willingness to take a chance on students like Jared. It's not worth that risk."

His hesitation was so brief she wondered if she'd imagined it. Then he punched in 911. "I'm not taking chances with you, either. That's a threat." He gestured toward the car. "It has to be reported." Before she could respond, his call was answered, and while he provided the requested information, she stared at the warning. Instead of intimidating her, it strengthened her resolve to help Jared. If gang members were responsible for this, as David suspected, their plan had backfired.

"All right. Thanks." David flipped his cell phone shut and slipped it back in his pocket as he turned to Caroline. "An officer should be here within a couple of minutes." He scanned the parking lot, then nodded toward the building. "Why don't you wait inside?"

Her chin lifted a notch. "I don't run away from trouble, David. I'll wait here with you."

As he studied her in the shadowed light, noting the resolve in her squared shoulders, the determined look in her hazel eyes, the uncompromising line of her lips, he found himself admiring her strength and tenacity. No wonder she'd been such a good reporter.

But he found himself admiring other things, as well. The delicate column of her slender throat. Her classic cheekbones. The graceful line of her jaw. As a sudden gust of wind whipped a few strands of silky hair across her face, he was tempted to reach over and let them drift through his fingers. Instead, he watched, motionless, as she lifted her hand to brush them aside with a graceful gesture. In the distance, a flash of lightning zigzagged across the night sky, followed by the muted rumble of thunder. The clouds that had been gathering on the horizon must have moved closer, because the air was now charged with electricity. Soon the storm would break. If they didn't take evasive action, they would both be caught in it.

"Maybe we should both go inside where it's safe." His voice rumbled deep in his chest, just like the thunder, sending a little shiver down her spine.

Although she couldn't see the expression in his shadowed eyes, Caroline sensed David's intensity. Heard the rough timbre of his voice. Felt her own pulse leap in response.

And suddenly knew that nowhere with David would be safe.

Before she could find her voice, a police car turned into the parking lot.

"Too late," David murmured, his gaze holding hers captive.

His comment was rife with meaning. And she

couldn't agree more. But right now she needed to focus on the immediate problem. Her car. She could worry about everything else later. Forcing herself to turn away, she looked toward the police.

Two officers emerged from the patrol car and walked over to them. The older one withdrew a notebook. "Good evening, folks. I'm Officer Scanlon. This is Officer Lowe. I understand you reported some vandalism?"

"Right there." David pointed toward Caroline's car.

The two men examined the damaged car, then scanned the ground with their flashlights. "I take it this is your car, ma'am?" The younger officer directed his question to Caroline.

"Yes."

"Any guess on when this might have happened?"

"I took the car out at lunch. It was okay then."

"Any idea who might have done it?"

David stepped in and gave them a brief overview of the situation, then voiced his own suspicions.

"A gang-related crime, huh?" The older officer took a closer look at Caroline, recognition dawning in his eyes. "This isn't your first run-in with gang violence, is it, Ms. James? Looks like the forehead healed up just fine, though."

Caroline felt David's intent gaze on her even before he spoke. "What does that mean?"

Forcing a nonchalant tone into her voice, she lifted one shoulder in an indifferent shrug. "Remember that series I told you about, the one I did last year on gangs? Someone didn't appreciate it. This—" she lifted her hand to touch the hairline scar "—was the result of a rock thrown at a window in my condo. I just happened to be standing in the wrong place when it came through. A voice mail at work the next day confirmed that it was related to that series."

A muscle in David's cheek twitched.

"Lucky for you it didn't take out an eye," Officer Scanlon said.

If Caroline had been the victim of gang violence once already, David realized that it could easily happen again. This time with far worse consequences. "Aside from the vandalism, what about the threat in that warning?" he asked the policemen.

"It could end right here. Or they could follow through. There's no way to tell. The easy solution is to end the internship."

"No way." Caroline folded her arms across her chest. "I won't be intimidated."

"Look, Caroline, maybe we need to talk about this," David interjected.

She turned to him and planted her hands on her hips, her eyes fiery. "No. I'm not going to deny Jared this chance."

David understood her commitment to the teen. He felt the same way. And he wouldn't care if the threat had been directed to him. He'd be just as adamant about seeing the thing through as Caroline was. But he felt a whole lot different knowing that she was a target— and that he was the one who had put her in the line of fire. Yet her resolve was strong. He doubted whether he was going to be able to convince her to back off, as the warning had instructed.

Jamming one hand in his pocket, he raked the fingers of the other one through his hair as he turned back to the policemen. "Is there anything you can do to track down the person or persons responsible for the vandalism?"

"Very little. We could dust for prints, but experience tells me we won't find any. Even small-time crooks and street kids know better than to leave that kind of evidence. And there's nothing in the immediate area that could have been used to do this. Right, Mark?" He turned toward his partner, who had continued to search the ground. The man nodded.

"Okay. What about Ms. James's safety?" David persisted. "What can you do to protect her, assuming whoever scratched that into her car intends to follow up on the threat?"

"We'll beef up patrols here at night." He turned to Caroline. "Do you still live in the area?"

"Yes."

"What's the address?" He jotted it down as she recited it. "We can schedule a few more patrols past your home, too. Other than that, I would just advise that you use caution. Avoid dark places by yourself at night—including this parking lot. Play it safe. And if you have any concerns, don't hesitate to call us."

When the officers finished filling out their report and headed back to their car, David gave Caroline a worried look. "I don't feel good about this."

She didn't, either. But there was no way she was going to let him see her fear. He'd just press her to send Jared packing, and she had no intention of doing that. "Everything will be fine, David. I'll be careful."

"I still don't like it. Neither will Jared. He was going to pass up this program to ease his grandmother's mind when she was worried about his safety. I suspect he'll feel the same way about you once he knows his presence is putting you in danger."

"Then we won't tell him."

"We have to."

"No, we don't. There's a possibility this incident isn't even gang-related."

"You don't believe that."

"It's possible," she insisted, her chin lifting in a stubborn tilt. "Promise me you won't tell him, David."

There had been a few times in his life when David had been torn between two less-than-ideal options. This was one of them. There just wasn't a good answer. No matter what course they followed, he'd worry.

Sensing his indecision, Caroline played her trump card. "If you tell Jared and he drops out, you'll need to explain it to the board. And that won't do Uplink any good. Let's just let things ride for a while. My guess is that this will be the end of it."

Even though her tone was confident, Caroline wasn't sure she believed that. Judging by his face, David didn't seem to, either. But she knew how much Uplink meant to him. She hoped he'd go along with her in order to safeguard the program, if for no other reason.

After several seconds, he conceded her point and capitulated—with reluctance. "Okay. But you have to promise me that you'll use extreme caution, and that you'll report anything suspicious, no matter how insignificant it seems."

"Of course." Then, brightening her tone, she reached for her door handle. "I don't know about you, but it's way past my quitting time. I'm out of here."

He beat her to the handle, then held the door open while she slid into the driver's seat and put her tote bag on the floor beside her. "I'll follow you home. It sounds like you live pretty close. I bought a small bungalow in Brentwood, so it won't be out of my way."

Words of protest rose to her lips, but she stifled them. Considering he'd let her win on the Jared issue, it might be best not to push her luck. And lightening things up a bit wouldn't hurt, either. "Your mother would be proud of your good manners," she told him, forcing a smile to her lips.

David figured that was true. But as he shut her door with an instruction to wait on the side street while he retrieved his car, he knew that good manners weren't his only motivation for following her home. His reasons went far deeper than that.

When David had met with Caroline to pass on Michael's medallion, he'd hoped that whatever infatuation had plagued him for two and a half long years would fizzle out once he was back in her presence. It hadn't. And as he'd gotten to know her better, as she'd dropped her wall of resentment and worked with him to help Jared, his feelings had deepened. Over the past few weeks they had evolved to respect and admiration and an attraction based on far more than the hormones that had surely triggered his initial reaction to her. In fact, as time had passed, his infatuation had begun to move toward love. But he'd resolved to put his feelings on hold during the summer, as they worked with Jared. He'd never believed in mixing business and pleasure.

Besides, he still had guilt and loyalty issues to work through. How could he pursue his brother's fiancée? Wasn't that wrong, somehow? Even though he was gone, Michael cast a long shadow. And Caroline's love for his brother had been deep and abiding. If and when she was ready to love again, would she, too, think it odd to consider the brother of the man she'd planned to marry as a potential suitor?

None of those questions had easy answers. And David hadn't planned to focus on them yet. Not while they were involved in a business relationship. But things had changed tonight, when he'd discovered that Caroline was in danger. He'd have to stick a whole lot closer to her than he'd planned, and he wasn't sure how he could do that without tipping his hand about his feelings—far sooner than she might be ready to accept them. And far sooner than he was prepared to reveal them.

But if she was going to put herself in jeopardy, he didn't plan to let her face the danger alone. He had to get more involved. There was just no way around it.

And he also planned to pray. For both of them.

Chapter Ten

Caroline jotted a final notation on the layouts for the next edition of the paper, then forked the last spear of broccoli in her Chinese take-out dinner. At least one good thing had come out of the vandalism incident, she mused. For the past two Mondays, David had appeared at her office at about seven o'clock, dinner in hand for both of them, and planted himself at an empty desk with his laptop while she finished up for the day, explaining that he didn't like the idea of her being alone at the *Chronicle*. And he especially didn't like her walking to her car by herself at night. So he'd taken up the job of bodyguard for one night a week, providing dinner to sweeten the deal.

As it had turned out, his considerate gesture had been unnecessary. Nothing more had come of the incident. But Caroline hadn't minded his attention. Capping her pen, she glanced his way, tracing his strong profile as he gave the document in front of him his full attention.

During both visits he'd left her alone while she worked, saying that he didn't want to disturb her.

Yet he'd done just that.

Reaching up, Caroline fingered the medallion that rested near her heart. She'd started wearing it more often, to remind herself that her growing attraction to David was inappropriate. And perhaps to warn him to keep his distance. But she wasn't sure how much longer it would have the desired effect. On herself—or on David.

The fact was, Caroline's feelings for David were deepening. Even though she felt guilty about it, she couldn't put the brakes on the sudden acceleration in her pulse when David appeared, couldn't contain the rush of tenderness that swept over her when she looked into his caring, compassionate eyes, couldn't suppress the yearning that filled her heart when she was near him. Nor could she understand her reactions. She still loved Michael—a good, decent man who had taught her how to embrace life and who had added a zest to her days that had forever changed her outlook on the world.

But David was a good, decent man, too. Though the brothers' different approaches to life each had appeal and charm, more and more she was beginning to think that in the long term, over a lifetime, David's quiet, measured style suited her better. And that not only made her feel guilty, but also disloyal.

As if sensing her scrutiny, David looked her way. For a brief second his eyes darkened, sending a rush of warmth to her cheeks. When he rose and walked toward her door, her lungs stopped working and a tingle of anticipation raced up her spine. He paused on the threshold, his gaze flickering down to her hand, which gripped the medallion around her neck, before it moved back to her face. For several seconds he just looked at her.

"I'm going to get some water. Would you like some?" he asked at last.

The innocuous comment was so at odds with the intense look on his face that it took her a second to regroup. "N-no, thanks. I should be done here in another twenty minutes."

"No rush. Take your time."

As he disappeared, Caroline's lungs kicked back into gear. She'd dated enough men to recognize David's expression. If it were anyone else, she'd have expected something to follow that look. A touch, perhaps even a kiss. But since David had never exhibited any romantic inclinations, maybe she was wrong. Maybe she was jumping to conclusions. Maybe her assessment of what had just transpired was simply wishful thinking. Whatever it was, though, she needed to get her emotions under control and stay at arm's length. She didn't need the kind of complication in her life that a romance with David would bring.

When he reappeared a few minutes later and went back to work, Caroline tried to ignore him. During her years composing copy in noisy, chaotic newsrooms, she'd learned to tune out distractions and stay focused. Yet those skills deserted her now. Like it or not, David was one big distraction. Finally, realizing that she was just spinning her wheels and wasting both their time, she reached for her tote and rose.

When she appeared at her door, David looked up in surprise. "Ready so soon?"

"Yes. I'll finish up tomorrow."

"You're not rushing because of me, are you?"

Yes. But not for the reasons you think. "No. It's just been a long day. What's left can wait until tomorrow."

"Okay." He swept his papers into a neat pile and slid them into his briefcase, then stood and followed her to the back exit. After she tapped in the code to set the night alarm system, they stepped out into the July heat.

"I didn't realize St. Louis was so muggy in the summer." David reached up to loosen his tie, giving the parking lot a quick but thorough scan as he walked with her toward her car.

"This is just a preview. Wait until August."

"That's encouraging."

She chuckled. "It does take some getting used to. Especially if you're from a place like Chicago that has a more reasonable climate in the summer."

"I prefer your winters, though."

"We've been lucky the past few years." Caroline was grateful for the small talk. It was easier to deal with than more personal subjects. And safer.

As usual, he opened her door, and she reached in to put her tote bag on the passenger seat before thanking him. But the words died in her throat when she straightened up and once more caught the unguarded look in his eyes. For the briefest second, she saw a warmth that made the July heat seem tame. A warmth suffused with yearning that told her in no uncertain terms that she wasn't alone in the attraction she'd been feeling. Unfortunately, she had no idea how to deal with that revelation. Or this situation.

David stared at the woman beside him, just inches away, and his fingers itched to reach out to her. To stroke her silky skin. To pull her close and wrap her in his arms. To protect her and shield her and love her. That urge had been growing stronger every time he was in her presence. And he was losing his battle to keep his distance, to maintain control.

But not tonight, he told himself, shoving his hands in the pockets of his slacks before he did something with them that he'd regret. He'd already revealed too much in the office a few minutes before, when he'd looked up to find her watching him. The temptation to touch her had been so strong that he'd actually walked to her office. Only the medallion around her neck had stopped him. The message it communicated, to back off, was as clear as the one that had been scratched onto her car two weeks before. Meaning that moving too soon would be a mistake. One that he might not be able to fix. And he wasn't about to take that chance.

"I'll follow you home." He tried to keep his tone conversational, but his voice was uneven, at best.

Instead of speaking, she just turned and slipped into her car. He shut the door and then headed for his own car a couple of spots away. And as he slid into the driver's seat and put his key in the ignition, he knew that one of these days, despite his best efforts, he was going to have to follow his heart. He just prayed that the Lord would give him restraint until the time was right.

* * *

In the days that followed, Caroline found her thoughts straying far too often to David. Her concentration slipped, and she wished she could focus on something—anything—except the man with the compelling, deep brown eyes.

Two weeks later, when the phone rang one afternoon in her office, she got her wish. And was sorry she'd ever made it.

"There's a bomb inside the *Chronicle*. You've got fifteen minutes to get out."

The muffled voice on the other end of the phone was almost indecipherable, but the message came through loud and clear. Caroline sprang to her feet, stabbing in 911 with a shaking finger even as she rose.

As soon as her call was answered she spoke, struggling to keep her voice steady. "This is Caroline James, managing editor at the *County Chronicle*. The paper has just received a bomb threat. The caller said the bomb would go off in fifteen minutes."

"We'll dispatch a bomb squad immediately. Evacuate the building and move away from the perimeter walls. The police should be there within a couple of minutes. Call back from a secure location if you need more instructions before then."

"Okay. Thanks." Caroline severed the connection, then called each of her department heads to relay the information and to ask that they make sure all of their people left the building. By her third call, there was already a flurry of activity outside her office as staff members began to rise in panic and rush toward the exits. When she finished the last call she grabbed her tote, pulling her cell phone out as she headed for her office door.

"Tess!"

Her assistant editor stopped in mid-flight, then hurried toward Caroline. The color had drained from her face, and she looked as shaken as Caroline felt. "Aren't you leaving?" Tess asked.

"Yes. But I'm going to do a walk-through first to make sure everyone's out. The police and bomb squad are on the way. Will you talk to them until I get out there?"

"Sure."

"Okay. Now go."

Caroline did a rapid inspection of the office. Only when she was convinced that everyone was out did she head for the door, tapping in David's office number as she strode through the lobby toward the front door.

"David? Caroline. We've had a bomb threat."

She heard the crash of a chair, as if David had jumped to his feet. "What!?"

"We've had a bomb threat. The police and bomb squad are on the way."

"Are you safe?"

"I'm leaving the building now."

"I'm on my way."

"Look, you don't need to come. I just wanted you to know."

"I'll be there in fifteen minutes. Are you out yet?"

She pushed open the front door and stepped into the late-afternoon sunlight. The police had already blocked off the street and seemed to be evacuating the surrounding buildings. Employees and curious onlookers were gathering in a parking lot across the street, and Caroline headed in that direction. "Yes. I just walked out the door."

"Okay. I'll see you in a few minutes."

By the time David arrived, Caroline had spoken to both the police and the bomb squad. She'd also dismissed the staff. It was late, and she doubted whether they'd get back inside before the workday ended. A lot of staffers were hanging around, though, including Jared. And news crews from the local TV stations were also arriving.

Weaving his way through the crowd, David made a beeline for Caroline. When he reached her he grasped her upper arms, relief flooding his features. "Are you okay?"

"Of course."

But she didn't look okay. Her face was drained of color, and he could feel the tremor in her muscles beneath his fingertips. Like the besieged rudder on a storm-tossed boat, his resolve to keep his distance snapped and he pulled her into his arms, pressing her close. Only then did he truly believe she was safe. It took every ounce of his willpower to finally release her and take a step back. "What happened?"

She stared at him, wide-eyed, as if the embrace had thrown her even more off balance. "A—a threat was called in. He said it would go off in fifteen minutes. That was twenty minutes ago."

"So it was a hoax?"

"I guess so. But they're not treating it that way." She inclined her head toward the police activity on the other side of the yellow tape that had been used to rope off the area.

"I would hope not. Has anyone given you an update?"

"Officer Scanlon is here. About five minutes ago he told me that they hadn't found anything yet. And they asked me a lot of questions about the security system." She looked toward Jared, still standing off to one side, then moved closer to David and lowered her voice. "Based on the incident with my car, the police seem to think this may be gang-related, too. They want to talk to Jared."

David had come to the same conclusion. And he was sure Caroline had, too, or she wouldn't have felt it necessary to call him right away. He looked over at the teen, who was still watching the activity from the sidelines, before turning his attention back to Caroline. "I can understand their concern. They probably think this is another intimidation tactic." He raked his fingers through his hair and fisted one hand on his hip. "This incident isn't going to be as easy to downplay as your car."

Surveying the TV cameras, Caroline nodded. "I know. But we don't have to tell the media about the potential gang tie-in. The police will be discreet, too, unless they find some direct evidence linking this to gang activity. And I doubt they will."

Caroline's cell phone began to vibrate, and she reached for it distractedly, her attention still focused on the scene before her. But when she answered it, she realized that the caller was the same person who had made the bomb threat, and her grip tightened, turning her knuckles white.

"This was just a warning. Next time it will be for real unless you get rid of Jared," the muffled voice said before the connection was severed.

As a look of shock passed across Caroline's face, David's eyes narrowed. "What's wrong?" When she didn't respond, he gripped her arms again, pinning her with an intense gaze. "Caroline, what's wrong?"

"It…it was the same person who called earlier. He said this was j-just a warning, but that next time it would be for real. Unless I get rid of Jared."

David's face grew hard, and he led her over to a low wall at the edge of the parking lot, urging her down as he motioned for a nearby officer. When the man joined them, David spoke. "Ms. James just had another call from the person who issued the bomb threat."

The man turned and gestured to another policeman, just as a reporter from one of the local TV stations honed in on them, camera crew in tow.

"Ms. James? Angela Watson, KMVI. Could you tell us what's going on?" The woman shoved a microphone in Caroline's face.

"I have no comment right now."

"We see bomb-sniffing dogs. Was there a bomb threat?"

"The police are still investigating. It would be premature to comment."

When the woman started to ask another question, David stepped between her and Caroline. "The lady said she has nothing further to say right now."

The reporter gave him a venomous look, then stalked off. When he was sure she didn't intend to return, David sat beside Caroline and reached for her ice-cold hand, twining his fingers with hers and giving them an encouraging squeeze. Although her responses to the reporter had been composed and professional, the trembling he'd felt earlier had increased. "Hang in there, okay?"

She tried to summon up a smile. "Yeah."

Several police officers gathered around as Caroline relayed the latest message.

"We'll continue to sweep the building, but my guess is there's nothing inside—this time," Officer Scanlon said. "And now that the caller has tied this to your intern, we need to talk to him as soon as possible."

"But he cut his gang ties weeks ago," Caroline said.

"Maybe. But even if he did, it's clear that his presence at the *Chronicle* still poses a risk."

She couldn't argue with that. It appeared she and David might lose their gamble with Jared after all—through no fault of the teen's. If the threat had remained directed just against her, Caroline wouldn't budge. But she had dozens of staff members to worry about. She couldn't endanger them. And David couldn't endanger the entire Uplink program for one student, no matter how talented he was.

Caroline faced the officer. "So are we just supposed to let that gang scare us into submission?"

"I don't like it, either, ma'am," he replied. "Why don't you let us check out your security system? If it's adequate, and if your staff is on high alert and no strangers are allowed in without proper clearance, there's little chance that a bomb could be placed inside. We'll also check out your maintenance crews. That could be a weak spot. If everything looks clean, you'll probably be okay."

It was the "probably" that gave her pause. And another quick glance at David confirmed that he felt the same way.

"I don't like playing the odds," he said, a frown creasing his brow.

"You folks will have to make that decision, based on our evaluation. In the meantime, I'd like to talk to your intern."

"He's right over there." David nodded toward Jared. "Can you let me lead off? We didn't tell him about the car incident, so he has no clue that any of this is related to him."

"Sure."

As David rose and motioned Jared over, Caroline stood and noted the curious looks being directed at the teen as he wove his way through the crowd. She turned to the officer. "Could we have this discussion somewhere in private?"

The policeman gave the scene a rapid survey, then pointed toward an insurance office a couple of stores down. "I know the owner there. I'm sure he'll let us use his conference room. Let me check it out."

As the man strode down the sidewalk, Jared joined them. His body was stiff with tension, and there was a look of caution on his face. "What's up?" he asked.

"The police have a few questions," David told him, placing a hand on his shoulder.

"What kind of questions?" Fear licked at the edges of his voice.

The officer reappeared on the sidewalk and motioned to them. "Let's talk about it in private," David suggested, leaving his arm around the boy's tense shoulders as he guided him toward the insurance company.

The small group remained silent until seated in the

conference room. David spoke first, his tone measured and nonaccusatory. "Jared, today's bomb threat was gang-related."

Surprise widened the teen's eyes before they narrowed in suspicion. "How do you know?"

"Ms. James just got another call, telling her that unless we let you go, there will be another threat. And next time it will be for real. This isn't the first incident, either. A couple of weeks ago, Ms. James found a warning scratched onto her car, telling her to back off. We weren't sure at the time that it was related to your internship, but this confirms it."

"I didn't have anything to do with any of this." Jared's tone was defensive, but fear etched his features.

"We believe you, Jared. But the police still have a few questions."

A bleak look settled over his face and he slumped in his seat. "I'm sorry I caused problems," he told Caroline.

"None of this is your fault, Jared," she assured him.

"At least as far as we can tell," Officer Scanlon qualified. As all three sets of eyes focused on him, he faced Jared and continued. "I understand you're trying to cut your ties to the gang."

"I did cut them."

"That's not easy to do."

"Yeah. Tell me about it."

When he didn't offer any more information, David stepped in, relaying the story of Jared's trip to the hospital.

"Is that right?" the officer asked Jared.

"Yeah."

"Why didn't you report it?"

The teen stared at him. "I already had two broken ribs. I didn't want more. Or worse."

After a moment, the officer gave a curt nod. "Okay. I know they play rough. I can appreciate your caution. But we're in a different league now. This bomb threat endangers dozens of people. We need information."

Jared swallowed. "I don't know anything."

"Names would help."

"Look, man, I've been out of touch with the gang for weeks. People come and go."

"Not the leaders."

Shifting in his seat, Jared looked from David to Caroline. The distress on his face was so agonizing that Caroline's heart ached for him. Reaching out, she covered his hand with hers. "We have to cooperate with the police," she said softly. "If we don't, the gang will win. And we'll all have to live in fear."

He looked down at her hand. He'd been in some tough situations, but this was one of the toughest. For most of his life he'd figured he didn't owe anybody anything, except maybe Nan. No one had ever done him any favors, given him a break. Sure, a couple of teachers at school had made him feel pretty good, had seemed to believe in him. But nobody had ever put themselves on the line for him like Mr. Sloan and Ms. James had. So he owed them. Giving the police the information they wanted was dangerous—for him. But he didn't see any way around it. Not if he wanted to be able to live with himself.

With an effort, he swallowed past the lump in his throat. Then he looked over at the cop. "Okay. I'll give you the names. But I'm not even sure they're still in charge. And even if they are, they're smart. You're not going to be able to tie them to this."

"Let us worry about that." Officer Scanlon flipped open his notebook and took out his pen, scribbling down the names as Jared ticked them off. "Okay. That's a start, anyway," he said when Jared finished. "We'll check them out. In the meantime, we'll do a security assessment of your facility," he told Caroline. "You might want to have people work from home tomorrow." He stood and tucked the notebook in his pocket. "I'll be in touch. And you did the right thing," he told Jared.

The boy drew a long, unsteady breath. "Yeah."

"We'll need you to hang around for a while," the officer told Caroline. "In case there are any other questions."

"Okay."

As he exited, David turned to Jared. "Can I give you a ride home?"

"No. I can still catch the bus." Without waiting for a response, Jared rose and walked toward the door, then looked back at Caroline. "So I should stay home tomorrow?"

"Yes. I'm going to contact all the staff members."

"What about the next day?"

"Let's wait and see what the police say."

At her noncommittal response, a weary resignation settled over Jared's face. "Okay. See you around."

As they watched him exit, Caroline's phone once more began to vibrate, and she reached for it automatically, her heart thudding in her chest.

"Another call?" David asked.

"Yes."

After she hit the Talk button and put the phone to her ear, she found her free hand taken in a firm, reassuring grip. David's powers to protect her were limited, but his strong hand holding hers calmed her, giving her an illusion of safety. It wasn't a good idea to let him hold her hand, of course. Not if she wanted to keep him at arm's length. But she couldn't summon up the strength to pull away.

"Caroline James."

"Caroline? I've been calling your office for an hour. I finally tried the receptionist but I couldn't get an answer there, either."

Closing her eyes, Caroline expelled a relieved breath. "Hi, Mom. We had to evacuate the building. There was a bomb threat."

"What?!"

"Everything's fine. It was a false alarm."

"What on earth prompted that?"

"It's a long story."

"All right. You can tell it to me at dinner. If you're still coming, that is."

With all that had happened, their weekly dinner date had slipped her mind. She checked her watch. Her mother always went to a lot of trouble to prepare a nice meal and she hated to disappoint her, but she wasn't sure how long she'd be delayed.

"I'd like to, Mom. But the police asked me to stay around for a while. And I have some things to discuss with David."

"Is he there?"

"Yes."

"Then this whole thing must have something to do with that young man from Uplink you told me about."

Her mother would have made a great detective, Caroline decided. "That's right."

"Well, he needs to eat dinner, too. I made plenty. Bring him along."

The suggestion startled Caroline, even as it tempted her. But spending a cozy evening with David at her mother's house wasn't a good idea. "I'm sure he has other plans, Mom."

Tilting his head, David gave her a quizzical look.

"You don't know that unless you ask him," her mother persisted.

"Is she asking about me?" David inquired in a soft voice.

Nodding, Caroline spoke into the receiver. "Hold on, Mom." She touched the mute button, trying to figure a way out of this without lying. "I'm supposed to go over there for dinner. Mom thought you might like to come, but I know it's last minute, and I don't expect…"

"I'd love to," he cut her off. "I haven't had a home-cooked meal in a long time."

Caroline stared at him. Maybe he was just angling for a good meal. Considering that her hand was still held in his protective clasp, however, she knew she was just fooling herself. No doubt, his motivations were far more complicated than that. And she had a feeling her life was about to become a lot more complicated, too. But she didn't see any way around it.

Taking her finger off the Mute button, she spoke. "We'll be there as soon as we can, Mom."

"Great! I'll see you in a little while."

Her mother sounded pleased, Caroline thought, as she severed the connection. But no more pleased than David looked. The smile that lit his eyes warmed her all the way to her toes, and the gentle squeeze he gave her hand as they rose and headed back outside seemed to be part thank-you and part reassurance that everything would be okay.

But Caroline wasn't sure about that. Earlier, the bomb threat had scared her, making her afraid for her physical safety. Yet the fear she felt now was just as strong. Except this time it was her heart that was in peril.

It had been years since Caroline had prayed. And she wasn't sure why she turned to the Lord now. Maybe it was because David's quiet, deep faith had rubbed off on her. Maybe it was because she didn't know where else to go for help. Whatever the reason, she sensed a need for assistance from a higher power.

Lord, I haven't talked with You much in recent years, she prayed as David left her for a moment to speak with the two officers. *Life got pretty busy, and I let my faith lapse. I forgot that I need You. But now I realize that I do. Please help us through this situation. Help us find a way to protect everyone's safety without being forced to give up on Jared. He has so much to offer, and I'm afraid that if this opportunity falls through, he'll end up on the street.*

And please help me deal with my feelings for David. I don't want to be disloyal to Michael, but David is so kind and caring and wonderful. And he's here, Lord. Michael always believed in living today without being constrained by the past. I think he'd want me to move on. It just seems awkward—and wrong, somehow—to move on with his brother. Please help me figure out how to deal with this situation. Because I don't want to pass up a second chance for love.

Chapter Eleven

"That was a wonderful meal, Mrs. James. Thank you again for inviting me."

"Please, call me Judy," Caroline's mother told David, who stood as she picked up the creamer. "And it was my pleasure. We were due for a little male companionship at one of our weekly tête-a-têtes. Overdue, in fact." She gave Caroline a pleased smile—one of the many she'd sent her daughter's way during the meal. A meal that had been served in the dining room—on the good china—instead of their usual spot in the kitchen or on the patio. "Now I know you and Caroline have things to discuss about Jared. You just sit here and get on with it while I load up the dishwasher."

"I'll help, Mom."

Caroline started to rise, but Judy put a hand on her shoulder. "Not tonight. You two have some decisions to make."

Although her mother had listened with interest as

Caroline and David spoke at dinner about Jared and the threats that had been issued, in an uncharacteristic display of reticence she'd made few comments and offered even fewer opinions. While Caroline sometimes found her mother a little *too* opinionated, she valued her insights and was curious about her take on the whole situation.

"What do you think about all this, Mom?" she asked, settling back in her seat.

Shaking her head, Judy reached for the butter dish. "It's an unfortunate situation. Jared sounds like a bright, talented young man who's trying to improve his life. But that gang is treacherous. I'd be lying if I said I wasn't worried. About everyone. And about you in particular." A spasm of distress tightened Judy's features as she looked at her daughter. "But I worried about you in the Middle East, too. I guess I'm used to it by now. And I've always been proud of your sense of justice and integrity, and your willingness to stand up for what you believe in. Those are some of the reasons I love you so much. I just hope you'll be careful." She turned to David. "What do *you* think?"

The look he gave Caroline was steady and sure. "I couldn't have said it any better."

A satisfied look settled over Judy's face. "That's what I figured. In the meantime, I guess I'll just keep bending the Lord's ear, like I did when you were in the Middle East."

As her mother bustled out of the room, Caroline stared at David. Had he just implied that he loved her? Or was he just agreeing with her mother's comment about being careful?

Instead of continuing that discussion, however, David switched topics. Steepling his fingers, he leaned forward, his face intense. "Your mother was right about Jared. We need to make some decisions."

Caroline exhaled a relieved breath. "I know. But I think we should wait until the police assess the security risk at the *Chronicle*. I don't want to give up on him yet. What about the Uplink board's reaction to all this?"

Twin furrows appeared on David's forehead. "As it happens, we have a regular board meeting tomorrow morning. I'm not sure how detailed the news coverage on the bomb threat will be, and I doubt Jared will be mentioned. But I owe it to the board to explain the situation. I had resistance from the beginning on taking high-risk students, and I need to be honest about the situation. However, I'm going to suggest that the board not take any action until we get the police assessment of the security risk."

"Do you think the members will go along with that?"

"I have no idea. But I'm going to pray that they do. Uplink needs to be there for students like Jared. Otherwise, it's not doing justice to its mission. Assuming the police come back with an encouraging report, how do you feel about keeping him on in light of all that's happened?"

"As long as I can be assured that danger to the staff is minimal, I plan to see this through."

"What about the danger to yourself?"

"I've been in dangerous situations before."

No doubt that was true. But it didn't make David feel a whole lot better.

At the odd expression on his face, Caroline tilted her

head and gave him a curious look. "Are you having second thoughts?"

"Not about helping Jared. I just never expected things to escalate like this. I thought we might have some trouble from Jared himself, but I didn't think the gang would bother him once he moved."

"Gangs don't look kindly on deserters. I learned a whole lot about how they operate when I did that series last year for the *Chronicle*."

"The one that earned you this." He leaned over and traced a gentle finger along the scar at her hairline.

She stared at him, trying in vain to stifle the sudden yearning that sprang to life at his touch.

"If you knew that much about gangs, I'm surprised you took Jared on." His voice was as soft as the finger that still rested against her temple.

"H-he deserved a chance."

"But the stakes are a lot higher now."

"I'm not a quitter, David."

He already knew that. But while he admired her commitment, it was playing havoc with his peace of mind. Knowing he was taking a risk, knowing it might be too soon, he reached for her hand, enfolding her fingers in his without ever breaking eye contact.

Her own eyes widened in surprise, and a pulse began to beat frantically in the hollow of her throat, but she didn't pull away.

"Caroline, I have to be honest with you. I'm having a real problem dealing with the danger you're in as a result of your involvement with Uplink—an involvement I initiated. The fact is, my feelings for you have…"

"Did I leave the lid for the butter dish on…" In one quick but comprehensive glance Judy took in the scene at the table, then turned on her heel. "I'll check later," she said over her shoulder, disappearing into the kitchen.

Caroline didn't know whether to be grateful or dismayed at her mother's interruption. But she did know that she wasn't ready to hear whatever David had been about to say. Giving her hand a gentle but firm tug, she pulled free from his grasp. "I'll be fine, David. But I appreciate your concern."

As she reached up to touch Michael's medallion, David drew a slow, steadying breath. Her message was clear. She wasn't ready yet to hear what he had to say. So he'd have to wait to tell her what was in his heart. But in the meantime, he was still going to worry.

After checking his watch, he rose. "I think I'll head out. It's been a long day. If you're ready to leave, why don't I follow you home?"

"I'm going to stay awhile and visit with Mom. But you go ahead. You need to be rested for your confrontation with the board tomorrow."

"I hope it won't come to that."

"I hope not, either. But you need to be in fighting form, just in case," she said with a smile.

"You're probably right." He rose, reaching for their plates.

"Leave the dishes, David. Mom and I will take care of them."

"Nope. I always clean up my own messes. Just lead the way to the kitchen."

Considering the firm set of his jaw, Caroline decided

arguing would be fruitless. She pushed through the swinging door, with David close on her heels, and Judy turned from the sink when they entered.

"He insisted on helping clear the table," Caroline told her.

"That's very nice. But not necessary."

"Many hands make light work. I'll bring in the rest of the dishes while you two ladies straighten up out here."

A few minutes later, when the table was cleared and the dishwasher loaded, they walked with him to the front door.

"Thank you again for a lovely evening, Judy. I haven't had such a good meal in a long time."

"It was my pleasure. You're welcome anytime."

"I'll remember that. Good night."

They watched as he headed down the front walk, returning his wave when he lifted a hand in farewell before striding toward his car. As her mother closed the door, she turned to Caroline. "He's quite a man."

"Yes, he is. But don't get any ideas."

"Considering the cozy scene I interrupted in the dining room, I don't think I'm the one with ideas."

A flush suffused Caroline's face. "All right. Let me rephrase my response. Don't get your hopes up. Whatever you saw isn't going anywhere."

"Why not?"

"Because I loved Michael. I still do."

"I feel the same way about your father. My love for him didn't die when he did. But that doesn't mean I can't also find room in my heart for someone else. Like Harold."

"That's different. Harold wasn't Dad's brother."

Her mother gave her a speculative look. "You know, back in Biblical times, it was very common for a man to marry his sister-in-law if his brother died."

"That was centuries ago."

"Good ideas never go out of style."

Propping her hands on her hips, Caroline stared at her mother. "Are you suggesting that I should *marry* David?"

"Only if you love him."

"I hardly know him!"

"Baloney."

"Okay, I guess I know him pretty well," Caroline conceded. "But there's nothing romantic between us."

"Hmph. You can believe that if you want to. But I saw the way you two looked at each other tonight. My body may be older, but my heart's still young and my eyesight is just fine. I know attraction when I see it. And I'll tell you something else. David may be Michael's brother, but he's also a keeper. I'd think long and hard before I discouraged his attention." With that, Judy headed back toward the kitchen.

If she could have mustered an argument, Caroline would have. But her mother was absolutely right. One day soon Caroline would have to deal with the thing simmering between her and David. She just wasn't yet ready to do so.

Mark Holton banged the gavel and called the Uplink board meeting to order. "David asked to be first on the agenda today because of an urgent issue that has arisen. We'll push the publicity report to second place, if that's okay with you, Rachel."

"Sure. No problem."

"David, you have the floor."

Standing, he faced the board. He could count on Steve to back him up. The rest he wasn't as sure about. But he wasn't going to back down—even if it put an end to his fledgling career. *Give me the right words to touch their hearts, Lord,* he prayed. *Help me make them understand that taking Jared on wasn't a mistake, even if it's put us in a difficult position. That helping kids like him is what we should do, even if it involves risk.*

"I don't know if any of you caught the late news last night, or read the paper yet this morning. If you did, you might have seen the story about the bomb threat at the *Chronicle,*" he began.

Several heads nodded, and Allison spoke. "I noticed it because the *Chronicle* is one of our new sponsoring organizations."

"That's right. Jared Poole is working there this summer," David confirmed. "And that's what I'd like to talk about this morning."

For the next few minutes, David gave them an overview of the situation, beginning with Jared's successful internship and ending with the final threatening call Caroline had gotten yesterday, along with the security review being done by the police. As he spoke, the expressions in the room changed from curious to uneasy to anxious.

"None of this information has made the press, and there's been no connection drawn between Uplink and the bomb threat. At this point, my recommendation is that we withhold action pending the police report.

Assuming the security at the *Chronicle* checks out, I'd like to let Jared complete his internship," he finished.

The board members exchanged nervous looks, but remained silent.

"I'm not anxious to put anyone in danger, David," Mark spoke up.

"I'm not, either. That's why I think we need to wait until we have the police report before we make a decision. But I wanted to brief all of you on the situation."

"Rachel, you're our publicity expert. What's your assessment of the long-term implications if the connection leaks?" Mark asked.

"Depends on how it's spun. We don't want to come across as a reckless organization that makes arbitrary decisions about the students we select and puts our hosting organizations in danger. On the other hand, if Jared is a success story, we could generate some great press for the positive impact Uplink has had by taking a few risks."

"Allison...what about the reaction of other hosting companies?" Mark asked the liaison chairperson.

"No company is going to want its operations disrupted or its employees put in danger. This could be a problem if more details leak or something else happens. What's the reaction at the *Chronicle?*" She directed her question to David.

"Caroline James, the managing editor, isn't easily intimidated. And she believes in Jared. At the same time, she's concerned about putting her staff at risk. She's agreed to wait until we have the security evaluation from the police before taking any action."

"Not every organization would be that cooperative," Mark noted.

"I realize that," David replied.

For the first time, Steve spoke. "I think the course of action that David has outlined is prudent."

"But there's still a risk," Mark pointed out. "Even if the police evaluation comes back positive and the *Chronicle* continues with the internship, there's no guarantee that something else won't happen. This gang seems to be persistent. And based on the attack on Jared, the members aren't averse to violence."

"I can't argue with that," David responded. "There is some risk. And there are no water-tight guarantees. But if we allow ourselves to be intimidated, we'll be closing Uplink to all the Jareds of the world. And compromising the integrity of the program."

"It's a tough situation. I think we're going to have to take a vote." Mark looked around the table. "All in favor of David's recommendation, raise your hand." Four hands went up—a couple with less-than-encouraging confidence. "All in favor of pulling Jared out of the program now, raise your hand." Three hands rose. "Let the record show that the vote was four to three in favor of continuing with the program given a limited-risk assessment by the police. You win, David. Just keep us apprised of the situation. We can call an emergency board meeting if necessary, should things change. Rachel, you're up."

As he took his seat, David expelled a relieved breath. But as for winning…he wasn't sure about that. Although the board had sided with him, the margin had been slim.

It was pretty clear that he was on thin ice. If much more weight was brought to bear, he suspected his support would give way and he'd go under—perhaps taking the Uplink program with him.

He just prayed that if that happened, no one would get hurt in the process. Especially the woman who had stolen his heart.

"Caroline James called. She said it was urgent."

That wasn't the kind of message David had hoped to be greeted with when he arrived at his office after the board meeting. His adrenaline, which had almost returned to normal since the charged meeting had ended, shot back up as he strode toward his office.

"How long ago?" he asked Ella over his shoulder.

"About half an hour. I said I'd have you call the minute you came in."

"Thanks."

He shrugged out of his suit jacket, tossed it onto the conference table and loosened his tie as he punched in Caroline's number. "What's up?" he asked as soon as she answered.

"David? How did the board meeting go?"

"They're with us. For now. Ella said your call was urgent."

"Yes. I heard from Jared this morning. He wants to withdraw from the program."

Sucking in a deep breath, David dropped into his chair and raked his fingers through his hair. If every internship was fraught with this much difficulty those few flecks of silver he'd noticed at his temples last week would spread as fast as weeds in a spring lawn. "What's the story?"

"He said he didn't want to cause any more trouble for anyone. And I think he was really shaken by the realization that if the gang follows through on its threat, a lot of people could be hurt."

"Did you hear anything from the police yet?"

"So far, so good. We've always had a first-rate security system, which the police verified. And they seem pretty comfortable that at least in terms of a bomb threat, we should be safe—especially if we follow our access security protocol. They're still checking out the maintenance crew, but it doesn't sound like that will be an issue, either. I'll have the final report this afternoon."

"Does that mean you're willing to see this through?"

"Yes."

"Okay. Then we need to talk with Jared."

"He sounded pretty firm."

"Let me give him a call. I'd like to get him into my office this afternoon, maybe with his grandmother, even his great-aunt, and talk this through. Could you join us?"

"Of course. Just let me know the time."

"All right. I'll be in touch."

The grim faces of those squeezed around his small conference table that afternoon didn't offer David much confidence that his persuasive skills would be effective. But after all the effort he'd expended getting Jared into the program, he wasn't about to let him walk away without a fight. And based on Caroline's determined expression, neither was she. At least he had one ally in the group.

Jared, on the other hand, looked beaten. His grandmother seemed sad. His great-aunt was a new player, and David studied her for a few seconds. She bore a faint resemblance to her sister, but she was dressed more upscale, in a tasteful linen suit. Her ebony hair was coiffed in a contemporary style, and her polished fingernails made it clear that her hands spent little time immersed in detergent—in sharp contrast to her sister's chapped, work-worn hands. Although she carried herself with poise and confidence, fear lurked in the depths of her eyes.

This wasn't going to be an easy sell.

"Can I offer anyone a soft drink?" David asked.

When everyone declined, he took his seat and directed his opening comments to Jared. "A lot of people have gone to a lot of effort and taken a lot of risk to help you succeed, Jared. Including those in this room. Before we write this internship off, I thought all of us should talk it through."

"There's nothing to talk about. I've already decided to drop out."

"Why?"

"Like I told Ms. James, I don't want to cause any more trouble."

"So you're going to let the gang win?"

"No. I'm not going to rejoin."

"But you *are* going to let them deprive you of an opportunity that could change your life forever."

"So what do you want me to do?" Jared demanded,

frustration nipping at the edges of his voice. "Stay and put everyone in danger?"

"We're still waiting for the final report from the police, but Ms. James has spoken with them. We're pretty sure they're going to conclude that security at the *Chronicle* is sufficient to reduce the risk of an actual bombing to almost zero."

"That doesn't mean the gang won't try something else. Hurt someone else. They already warned Ms. James. Maybe next time it will be Nan. Or Aunt Dara. Or even you."

"David and I are willing to take that risk." Caroline glanced at David as she spoke, then looked back at Jared. "And I have a feeling your grandmother feels the same way."

"I don't care how she feels. The apartment's not safe. It would be too easy for the gang to hurt her."

"Then she'll just have to come and stay with me." At Dara's statement, everyone turned to her in surprise. She looked back at them, tilting her chin up a notch. "Well, why not? I have two empty bedrooms. My neighborhood is secure. It's the best solution."

There was a suspicious sheen in Grace's eyes as she reached over and took her sister's hand. "You've already done more than enough for us. We couldn't ask you to take this on, too."

"You didn't ask. I offered." She leaned forward, her face intent, the fear in her eyes replaced by determination. "I want to do this, Grace. Besides, if we stick together, we can protect each other. There's safety in numbers, remember? And there's a nice young police officer who lives next door to me. He'll watch out for us, too."

"Are you sure about this, Dara?"

"More sure than I've been about most things in my life."

"Jared?" Grace looked at her grandson.

"I guess…I guess that would be okay." He turned toward David and Caroline, his face puzzled. "Since Nan and Aunt Dara are family, I can kind of understand why they're willing to take a chance for me. But I still can't figure out why you are."

"This is what Uplink is all about, Jared. Taking a chance on teens who have talent and potential. And from a personal standpoint, it's just the right thing to do. The Lord said to love one another, and I can't think of a better way to demonstrate that love than by giving a deserving young person a helping hand."

"We're also repaying a debt," Caroline added softly, her gaze flickering for a brief second to David. "A stranger once helped a man we both loved get a start in life. That man always wanted to do the same for another young person. But he never had the opportunity. So we're doing it for him."

Looking from one to the other, Jared shook his head. "I don't know what to say."

"*Thank you* would be good," Nan prompted.

A grin tugged at the corners of Jared's mouth. "You always were a stickler for etiquette."

"We may be poor, but that's no excuse for bad manners."

"Yeah. Okay. Thanks," he said, directing his comment to David and Caroline.

"Is there anything else we should do?" Dara asked.

"Praying might not be a bad idea." David's somber demeanor underscored the seriousness of his suggestion.

"I've been doing that. But I'm going to do a whole lot more," Grace declared, making a move to stand. "Thank you both." She extended her hand to David and Caroline in turn. Dara and Jared did the same.

"I'll see you at the office tomorrow," Caroline told Jared.

"I'll be there."

As the three exited via the front door, Ella handed David a stack of messages. "These all came in during your meeting."

"No rest for the weary, I guess," he replied, flipping through them as he spoke.

Caroline retrieved her purse. "I need to be going, anyway."

"I'll walk you to your car."

"No need. I'm right in front." She pointed to her car, visible out the window. As Ella answered yet another call, Caroline motioned to the messages in David's hand. "It doesn't look like you'll be leaving for a while."

"I'm hoping I can get through these quickly. I'm meeting a friend for pizza tonight."

Caroline stared at him. It had never occurred to her that David might be dating someone. Of course, there was no reason he wouldn't have an active social life. He was a handsome, intelligent, caring man. Any woman would be happy to spend time with him.

Realizing that she had misinterpreted his comment,

David hastened to explain. "I might have mentioned Steve Dempsky to you once. The guy I went to college with, who's a minister now and is on the Uplink board. Sometimes when his wife travels, we meet for dinner. I see him every Sunday at church, but our dinners keep our friendship strong."

Relief coursed through her, reminding Caroline that she cared far more about this man than perhaps was prudent. "He's the pastor of your church, too?" It was an inane comment, but she didn't know how else to respond.

"Yes. He gives a great sermon. You'd be welcome to join us anytime. The congregation is very friendly, and you might find the experience worthwhile."

"Maybe I will. Well…" She consulted her watch. "I need to be off. Have a nice evening. See you later, Ella."

"You take care, honey," the woman responded.

From his position by Ella's desk, David was able to follow Caroline's progress toward her car. He couldn't help but feel encouraged by the shocked look on her face when she'd thought he had a date tonight. It had told him she cared for him at a far deeper level than she perhaps wanted to. But he was also aware that she was fighting the attraction, just as he was. They both still had issues related to Michael that they needed to resolve before they could move forward. But he was working on his. And he hoped she was working on hers. Until now, he'd been able to rein in his feelings and keep them under wraps. But it was an ongoing battle. One he figured he was going to lose sooner rather than later.

He turned to find Ella watching him, a knowing look on her face. "She is one sweet lady. But I guess I don't need to tell you that, do I?"

And as she turned back to her computer, David realized he'd already lost the battle.

"Listen, thanks for voting in my favor today." David reached for another slice of pizza as Steve took a swig of his soda.

"I just followed my conscience. But that doesn't mean I'm not worried."

"Me, neither. Caroline got the police report this afternoon, though, and the *Chronicle* security system got an A-plus. They think there's little chance that a real bomb could be planted."

"That doesn't mean the gang won't try something else."

It was the same concern Mark and Jared had voiced. And it was the same one that was keeping David awake at night.

"Yeah, I know." David put down the piece of pizza, his appetite vanishing.

"You realize you might be putting yourself in danger, don't you?"

"I can take care of myself. I'm more worried about Caroline, since she's already had a direct threat. I'm not sure I could live with myself if…" His voice choked, and he cleared his throat.

Leaning forward, Steve scrutinized David's face. "Do I detect more than professional interest here?"

David raked his fingers through his hair. "You and everyone else, it seems. I thought I was doing a pretty good job disguising it, but Ella's picked up on it. I think Caroline's mother has, too."

"What's wrong with that?"

Although he and Steve had been close for years, he'd never talked to his friend about his connection to Caroline. When he'd first met her, he'd been so over-whelmed—and guilt-ridden—by his attraction to his brother's fiancée that he hadn't discussed her with anyone, afraid that he'd reveal his inappropriate feelings. But maybe now was the time to bring it up. Especially since that original infatuation had mushroomed into full-blown love.

Reaching for his glass, he took a long swallow of soda, then gave Steve a direct look. "Caroline was Michael's fiancée."

Steve stared at him. "Your brother, Michael?"

"Yeah."

"But…I thought he was engaged to a reporter in the Middle East?"

"He was. Caroline worked for AP then. After Michael died, she came home to St. Louis."

"And you two kept in touch?"

"No. I didn't see her until I stopped in one day after I moved here to give her something of Michael's that had been returned to me with his personal effects. I never planned to see her again after that."

"Why not?"

"I'm not sure how to…it's just that I've always…ever since we met I…" He stopped and shook his head, gripping his glass with both hands. "Sorry. I've been struggling with this for more than two years. To use an old cliché, I've been carrying a torch for her since the first time I saw her."

"You mean you're in love with her?"

"I am now. Back then…I don't know. I guess it was infatuation. I've never believed in love at first sight."

"I never did, either. Until I met Monica."

"You fell in love with your wife the first time you met?"

"I don't know if it was love, exactly. But right away I knew she was something special. Since we got married eighteen months later, I guess my instincts were right. And I learned not to discount first impressions. Besides, what's the problem?"

"In a word…guilt."

A light dawned on Steve's face. "You feel disloyal to your brother."

"Bingo."

"He's been gone for more than two years, David."

"He wasn't when I first felt this way."

"You didn't do anything about it then, did you?"

"No. But I was tempted."

"Temptation is part of being human. The real test of our character and faith is whether we act on those temptations. You didn't."

"Are you saying it's okay to fall in love with my brother's fiancée?"

"Considering the situation, I don't see a big issue from an ethical or moral standpoint."

A couple of beats of silence ticked by. "There's more," David told him.

"I kind of figured there was. Want to tell me about it?"

A wry smile lifted one corner of David's mouth.

"This was supposed to be dinner, not a counseling session. You do enough of this during the day."

"I may be a minister, but I'm also your friend. And friends are there for each other. If you want to talk, I'll be happy to listen."

His role in Michael's death was something else David had kept to himself. Only Caroline knew about it. In many ways, that was even harder to talk about. But guided by Steve's quiet questions, he told him the story about their mother's rapid decline and the argument the night before Michael died, which had no doubt distracted his brother—and maybe even caused his death.

"So I feel doubly guilty about Caroline. Not only is there a good chance that I contributed to my brother's death, but now I want to claim the woman he loved," David finished.

"I see your dilemma," Steve sympathized. "Guilt can be a powerful force for good, when applied in the proper circumstances. But it can also hold us back or result in unnecessary self-denial when misapplied."

"Do you think that's what's happening here?"

"Only you can answer that question. But from what you've told me, I don't see how denying your love for Caroline is going to help anyone. Maybe your feelings for her were inappropriate when you first met, but since you didn't act on them, there's no reason for guilt. I can't say what role your argument played in Michael's death. Maybe none. No one will ever know. But blaming yourself for it for the rest of your life isn't going to bring Michael back. It may be time to give it to the Lord, ask

His forgiveness for any responsibility you might bear and then let it go."

"I've tried that. And I thought I'd made my peace with it. But when Caroline came back into my life, I realized the guilt was still there."

"Then try again. Ask the Lord to help you let it go, to lift the burden from your shoulders. Put it in His hands and move on with your life. With Caroline, if that's where your heart leads you. Assuming she feels the same way, of course. Does she?"

"I think so."

Reaching over, Steve laid his hand on David's shoulder. "Maybe it's time you found out."

Chapter Twelve

The organ music swelled, and for the dozenth time Caroline tried to figure out how she had wound up in church, beside David, on this bright August morning.

When he'd suggested earlier in the week, after their meeting with Jared and his family, that she consider attending his church, her response had been a polite, "Maybe I will." While she admired David's deep faith and felt a growing need to connect with a higher power herself, she'd made little effort to do so aside from a few recent prayers in the quiet of her heart. Life had just been too busy. But that had always been her excuse, she acknowledged. Finding time for God hadn't been one of her priorities during her hectic years with AP. She'd been too focused on building her career, surviving in new and sometimes hostile environments…and falling in love with a man for whom religion had never been top-of-mind. At best, Michael had been an agnostic. While he hadn't denied the existence of God, he hadn't bought into Christianity. Although Caroline had been raised Christian and still believed the basic tenets of the faith, she hadn't practiced it in any formal way for years. And except for an occasional sense that there was a spiritual emptiness in her life, she hadn't missed it.

But when she'd met David the Christmas she and Michael visited, she'd been intrigued by the sense of purpose his deep faith seemed to give to his life. And ever since then, she'd been drawn toward the source of that purpose. Vague at first, the call had grown steadily stronger after Michael's death. Though she'd done little to heed it, and in fact sometimes found it annoying, the quiet voice deep in her soul had persisted. As a result, when David had called yesterday and invited her to join him for services, she'd said yes.

While she'd been afraid that the situation between them might be awkward after that interrupted moment at her mother's house, David had worked hard to ease any tension, sticking to safe subjects and even eliciting a few laughs with a story about how Ella's plants were taking over their offices. By the time they arrived at the small brick church with the tall white steeple, she'd been relaxed and receptive to the experience.

So far, she'd enjoyed the service. Steve Dempsky had merry eyes and a ready smile—as well as a great singing voice that soared above the choir. He conducted the service with an infectious joy and enthusiasm that seemed to capture the true spirit of Christianity. Caroline had been concerned that she would feel self-conscious and ill at ease in church after such a long absence, but to her surprise the experience seemed more like a homecoming. It felt right to be back in the house of the Lord.

As the minister moved to the pulpit to deliver his sermon, Caroline aimed a sideways glance at David. He was focused on the sanctuary, giving her a good view of his strong, appealing profile. Although he came across as a composed, disciplined person who could be counted on to analyze any situation and make a sound judgment, Caroline suspected that beneath his calm, restrained exterior, David was a man of strong passion, whose feelings ran deep. She'd glimpsed that side of him once or twice when he'd looked at her in an unguarded moment. And on some intuitive level she knew that he was the kind of man who, when he loved, would give release to his feelings with such intensity that the mere thought of it took her breath away.

So captivated was she by these wayward musings that Caroline missed a good part of the minister's sermon. Only with great effort—fueled by guilt at her inappropriate thoughts in this house of God—did she shift her attention to the front of the church and focus on his words.

"And so I think that our reading today from Ecclesiastes will always remain timeless. To everything there is a season…that's just as true today as it was three hundred years before the birth of Christ, when this passage was written. Each of us has experienced seasons in our lives. Times of happiness and times of sadness. Times of putting down roots and times of pulling them up. Times of grieving and times of rejoicing. We know that there are times to be silent, and times to speak.

Times to draw close, and times to stay apart. As the author of Ecclesiastes reminds us, the Lord has made everything appropriate to its time.

"Those words are a great source of comfort. They help us understand that the ebbs and flows of life are natural, that we're not alone in the difficulties we encounter. But they also bring a challenge. Because they leave some of the choices about the seasons of our lives in own hands. Grief is a good example. While we don't choose our times to grieve, we do choose the duration of our mourning. Clinging too long to grief can blind us to other joys God sends our way. The same is true of hate. Clinging too long to this destructive emotion can harden our hearts. Likewise, clinging too long to baggage from our past can clutter our lives, leaving no room for anything new to enter."

The minister surveyed the congregation before him, his expression kind and compassionate. "My friends, while this passage provides a reassurance that we're not alone when we experience the diverse seasons of our lives, it also serves as a wake-up call. A reminder that sometimes it's up to us to step from one season into the next. To go from weeping to laughing, from scattering to gathering, from losing to seeking. And as we move through these seasons, we have one advantage the writer of Ecclesiastes didn't have: an understanding of the purpose and plan for our lives, which the Lord provided during His time on earth. We also have someone to turn to when we need guidance for our journey. When we need courage to choose a new season. Let us always remember the beautiful words from Matthew: 'Ask, and it shall be given to you; seek, and you shall find; knock, and it shall be opened to you.' The Lord waits for our call. Don't be afraid to ask Him for help as you journey through the seasons of your life.

"And now let us pray…."

As the minister continued with the rest of the service, the words of his sermon resonated in Caroline's mind. It was almost as if he'd looked into her heart and chosen a topic that would have special significance for her first visit back to church. His talk had captured many of the conflicts and feelings she'd been experiencing these past few weeks, since David had reentered her life. And it had made her question her doubts about pursuing a relationship with him. Was she clinging too long to grief? Was the baggage she was holding on to from her past robbing her of her future? Was it time to ask for forgiveness for the role she'd played in Michael's death and move on? Michael would want her to, she knew. And maybe the Lord did, too.

Bowing her head, she closed her eyes in prayer. *Lord, I listened to the words today from Your book with an open heart. And I listened to the minister as well. For the past two years I've been living in an emotional vacuum, consumed by grief and guilt and hate. I hated myself for the role I played in Michael's death, and I resented David for his role. I don't resent him anymore, Lord. And I'd like to stop hating myself. I want to move on. It's time. I've lived in the darkness of winter for too long. I want to move to the next season, to spring and the new life that will bring. A life that I'd like to share with David.*

I ask Your help, Lord, in making that transition. Please give me peace of mind about the decision, relieve me of the guilt I feel and give me the courage to enter this new season. I'll always love Michael, but as Mom told me recently, loving one person doesn't mean there's no room in your heart for someone else. I used to think that it was a coincidence that David's new job brought him here. Now I think maybe it was more than that. That maybe You brought him to me. And that You're leaving the next step to me. Please give me the courage to take it.

With trembling fingers, Caroline reached up and touched the medallion around her neck. It had served as an expression of her love and devotion to the man she'd planned to marry—and a warning to the man beside her to keep his distance. A warning David had respected. But it was time to remove the wall that had kept him away—and kept her safe. She knew that tearing it down would expose her to risk. Yet even though the wall had protected her, it had also isolated her, leaving her heart cold and dark and lonely. And more and more, her heart was yearning for sunlight and warmth.

Summoning up her courage, Caroline lifted her hands and sought the clasp behind her neck. Without giving herself time for second thoughts, she opened it, letting the medallion and chain slide into her waiting hand. And as she felt the weight in her palm and closed her fingers around it, the oddest thing happened. Though the sky had been dark and ominous when they'd arrived at church, a sudden shaft of sunlight darted through the stained-glass window beside her, painting her hand—

and only her hand—with a rainbow-hued mosaic of rich, bright, vibrant color. She froze, and her breath caught in her throat as she stared at it. Several seconds ticked by, and then David reached over and covered her hand with his. Startled, she turned to him. The tender expression on his unguarded face told her that he'd observed her symbolic maneuver, understood the significance—and approved.

And as she glanced down at his fingers, protectively covering hers, the mosaic of color seemed to deepen in intensity and expand to accommodate David's larger hand. Once more her gaze sought his. The pensive look on his face told her that he, too, was pondering the odd timing of that shaft of vivid light. And that like her, he wondered if, in this subtle way, Michael was giving them his blessing.

Caroline wasn't the type of person who believed in signs. She was too practical by nature, too much of a journalist, always wanting proof and impeccable sources. She was from the Show-Me state, after all. The play of light was probably just a coincidence, she told herself.

Yet deep in her heart, she sensed it was more than that. And all at once she experienced a feeling of release, of liberation. Of absolution, almost. Maybe it was just wishful thinking. But even so, the effect was the same. And bowing her head in gratitude, she uttered a silent prayer of thanks.

After one more quick scan of Jared's entry for the journalism contest, Caroline handed it over to the intern. "I'd say we're almost there. I just have a few more minor editing suggestions, and Bill has recommended some slight cropping revisions on the photos. See what you think."

As Jared dropped into a seat across from her desk and looked over his mentors' comments, Caroline leaned back in her chair and flexed her shoulders. With the deadline looming in two days, she and Jared had stayed far later than usual to finish the entry. It had been too hectic at the *Chronicle* to work on it during normal business hours. But she didn't mind putting in the extra time. Jared had written a stellar piece on the plight of residents at an underfunded nursing home, and his dramatic photos of the elderly inhabitants had reinforced his powerful words. Caroline had no doubt that he'd be a finalist, if not one of the winners.

Reaching for her bottle of water, she took a long sip, hoping to stem the hunger pangs in her stomach until David arrived in half an hour to take her out to dinner. A smile curved her lips at that thought. Since their church visit four days earlier, they'd had almost no time together. Just as the service ended, she'd been paged about a breaking story and had to leave right away for the office. David had been sequestered in wrap-up meetings all week with Uplink hosting organizations as the internships wound down. Plus, she'd been staying late for the past few days to work with Jared on his entry. But now that she'd resolved her issues, she was anxious to move forward with their relationship. To explore the opportunity that had blessed her life and see where it led. As a result, when David had suggested a late dinner, she'd responded with an immediate yes.

"These comments all make sense," Jared said, interrupting her thoughts. "I can make the changes before I leave. But you don't need to hang around to give me a ride home like you did the other nights. Aunt Dara said she'd come and get me if I needed to stay extra late tonight to finish this up."

"I don't mind. David and I are going to dinner, and he'll be swinging by at eight o'clock to pick me up. We can drop you off on our way to the restaurant."

Even if he wasn't coming by, Caroline wouldn't have left. While things had been quiet since the bomb threat, and Jared's internship would be over at the end of the following week, she wasn't confident that they'd heard the last of the gang. She figured there was safety in numbers.

Rising, Jared fingered the papers in his hand. "He's a good guy."

"Yeah. He is."

"I thought he was going to write me off after my first interview. I wouldn't have blamed him if he had."

"He recognized your talent and wanted to give you a chance to develop it."

"I guess. But I…I couldn't figure out why, in the beginning. Then I realized he was into the Jesus stuff, like Nan and Aunt Dara. And everything kind of fell into place at that meeting we all had, when I asked him why he was going out on a limb for me, and he said it was just the right thing to do. That he was following the Lord's commandment to love one another."

"I'd say that's a pretty accurate assessment of his motives."

"I think that's pretty cool, you know? I was never

much into religion, even though Nan dragged me to church when I was a kid. But nothing in my life ever convinced me there was really a God who cared about me. Then all this good stuff happened this summer. And people like you and Mr. Sloan and Mr. Baker believed in me." He looked down and shifted his weight. "Anyway, I started going to services with Nan and Aunt Dara. And I thought maybe you might want to tell Mr. Sloan. He never talked to me about going to church, but I think he might like to know, since it's so important to him."

A warm smile lighted Caroline's face. "I know he would. I'll be sure to pass it on."

"Thanks. Listen, these changes won't take long. Just give me ten or fifteen minutes."

"No rush. I have plenty to do here. And David's not coming for half an hour, anyway."

Twenty minutes later, with Jared still intent on his revisions, Caroline signed off on the last piece of copy in her review stack and reached for her purse. She still had time to pay a few bills before David arrived, and a couple of them were bordering on overdue. She'd just been too busy to get to them until now.

A quick search in her purse reminded her that she'd tucked her checkbook under the front seat of her car the day before—a bad habit she'd gotten into years before when she'd often traveled without a purse. One of these days she needed to correct that, she reminded herself.

"Jared, I'm going to run out to my car to get something. I'll be back in a couple of minutes," she called to the teen across the empty newsroom.

He swallowed the bite of sandwich he'd been chewing while he worked. "Okay. I'm almost done."

Pausing in the break room, Caroline pitched her empty water bottle and spared a quick glance in the mirror, reminding herself to apply some lipstick before David arrived. By the end of the day, every speck had usually vanished. Most of the time she didn't care. But tonight…well, tonight she cared.

Since the gang-related incidents, Caroline had been cautious, putting herself on high alert whenever she was alone—especially around the *Chronicle*. But as she pushed through the back door into the muggy, oppressive August twilight, her thoughts were so distracted by the evening ahead with David that she didn't notice the fragments of glass on the pavement next to the exit—all that was left of the security light. And she didn't see the two figures in the shadows until they lunged toward her.

By then, it was too late to do much. The hand clamped over her mouth stifled the scream that rose to her lips, and her arms were wrenched behind her with such force that she gasped in pain. On instinct alone, with no conscious thought, she used the only part of her body that was still unconstrained. With one swift kick, she slammed the door shut behind her, drawing some measure of relief when it locked with a decisive click. At least Jared would be safe inside. Thanks to the *Chronicle*'s heightened security, the electronic access card reader had been temporarily disabled. No one could enter from the outside without the security combination.

But her action drew the ire of her two assailants. Their faces were indistinct in the dusk, but she could tell they were young. One looked to be about fifteen or sixteen, the other perhaps a bit younger. The identical bands they wore on their arms beneath the cutoff sleeves of their T-shirts told her at once that they were associated with a gang.

"That wasn't very smart," one of the boys snarled, tagging on the same vulgar term that had been scratched into her car. "Open the door." They shoved her next to the keypad and released one of her arms. "We want Jared."

Fighting down her suffocating fear, Caroline tried to prod her paralyzed brain into action. She knew she couldn't open the door, couldn't expose Jared to the danger these teens represented. But the consequences of noncompliance sent a new wave of terror rippling through her.

"Open the door!" One of the teens twisted her arm, and the sharp pain that shot through her wrist bent her double. "Stand up and open the door." The pressure on her arm eased and she was pulled upright.

Please, Lord, help me! she prayed in desperation.

When she still hesitated, the younger thug grabbed a fistful of her hair, then slammed the side of her face against the metal door. For a second, pinpoints of light exploded behind her eyes, obscuring her vision. She sagged against her captor as a wave of dizziness swept over her.

"Hey, man, be careful. She ain't gonna be no use to us if she passes out."

"Yeah, well, we ain't getting nowhere this way."

"She must have an access badge. Hold on to her." The older of the two moved in front of her and put his face close to hers. "You gonna give it to us, or you wanna do this the hard way?"

When she didn't respond, his eyes narrowed. "Okay. You asked for it."

Caroline closed her eyes and tried not to cringe as his hands moved over her body in a rough and thorough pat-down.

"It ain't here," he pronounced when he finished.

"So whaddaya wanna do?" The younger kid was starting to sound nervous.

"I got an idea."

Although her vision was still slightly blurred, Caroline had no trouble identifying the shiny silver object he withdrew from his belt as a knife. The boy put the point to her throat and his face hardened. "Okay, you got ten seconds to open that door. If you don't, we're gonna keep doing this until you do." In a flash, he removed the point of the knife from her throat, pulled one arm from behind her back and slashed the blade down her forearm. Immediately blood began to ooze from the four-inch gash.

Stunned, Caroline stared at the wound. For a second she thought she was going to faint. Not from pain. So far she felt nothing. It was fear that caused her light-headedness. She'd been in some dangerous situations in her journalism career, but none where she was the intended victim. This was a whole different ballgame. There was no doubt in her mind that these two punks would follow through on their threat. Their expressions were cold, detached. As if hurting people—or taking a life—was no big deal. And maybe it wasn't, for them. That's what made this situation so terrifying.

"Let's try it one more time." The teen who had

produced the knife, the older of the two, gestured to the kid behind her, who once more shoved her face close to the keypad.

She had to do something. Stall, if nothing else. Maybe the police would come by. They'd been patrolling the area with increased frequency for the past few weeks. They could appear at any second.

Slowly she lifted her hand. The cut on her arm was bleeding more now, bathing her arm in red. But that was the least of her problems at the moment.

Taking as much time as she dared, Caroline punched in a set of numbers. The wrong numbers. A fact that became apparent to the two thugs when they tried the door and it didn't budge.

Once more, she was jerked around and her arm was yanked forward. "I guess we'll have to do some more persuading," the older boy sneered.

Just as he positioned the knife, the back door opened. All three heads swiveled toward Jared, who stood on the threshold, staring at the scene in shock. He must have come to check on her because she'd been gone for too long, Caroline realized, her panic escalating. In the next instant, she was shoved to the ground as the two youths sprang at the teen.

For a few seconds she lay unmoving, the breath knocked out of her. She was aware of a scuffle taking place, of the dull sound of fists hitting solid flesh, of grunts textured with pain, but little else registered. By the time she could react, the two youths had subdued Jared, who had fallen to his knees. Blood streamed from his nose, and his breathing was labored.

As she struggled to her feet and opened her mouth to scream, the older teen once more brandished his knife. "Make a sound and we'll finish him off right now."

She froze and looked over at Jared. There was fear in his eyes, but also anger. "I don't know these dudes." He spoke fast, in quick gasps. "But they're from my old gang…some kind of initiation rite."

"Shut up." The guy with the knife kicked him in the side—the side with the healing broken ribs. Caroline flinched and a wave of nausea washed over her, followed by a fresh surge of fear. She'd learned enough about gangs to know that initiation rites often involved senseless and random acts of violence.

"Now that we got the traitor, whaddaya wanna do with *her?*" The younger kid motioned toward Caroline.

"I don't know." The youth with the knife gave her a speculative look. When he spoke again, his tone was almost jovial. "But maybe two is better than one. Or even three, if someone else shows up."

David! He would be here any minute, Caroline realized with a jolt. If she didn't answer the front buzzer, he'd no doubt come around to the back. And walk right into this volatile situation. Just as Michael had done the day he died—also because of her. It was a replay of the nightmare that had haunted her for two years. She had to do something!

Catching Jared's eye, she inclined her head slightly to the guy beside him, with the knife. Then did the same toward the guy behind her. Judging by his nod, he got the message. They might not succeed in resisting their attackers, but it was better than waiting for these two thugs to finish them off. At least they'd go down fighting.

Jared was poised for her signal, his face frightened but resolute.

This is it, Lord, she prayed. *Give us strength and courage. Be with us no matter what happens.*

And with that, she nodded to Jared.

Chapter Thirteen

As he pressed the night bell for the second time, a tingle of unease raced along David's spine. He knew Caroline and Jared were here. He'd called Caroline less than an hour before to confirm their dinner date. Why wasn't she answering?

Once more, he pressed the bell—and held it. But again, there was no response. His apprehension escalated to alarm. Just as he reached for his cell phone to call 911, he spotted a police car on routine patrol heading his way. *Thank You, Lord!* David prayed as he flagged down the vehicle.

Officer Scanlon got out of the car as David approached. "Can I help you, sir?"

"David Sloan, officer. We met the day of the bomb threat. I had an appointment with Caroline James this evening, but there's no answer. She was here an hour ago and planned to meet me. Our Uplink intern, Jared

Poole, is with her." His tone was clipped and curt as he fought down his rising panic.

The policeman turned to his partner, who had emerged from the vehicle on the other side. David recognized Mark Lowe as well.

"Call headquarters and report suspicious activity at the *Chronicle*," Officer Scanlon instructed. "Request silent back-up. I'm going around to the rear. You cover the front."

Without waiting for a response, he withdrew his gun and took off at a trot toward the corner of the street, avoiding the alley. When David started to follow, he waved him back.

For a second, David hesitated. He wanted to do something to help. But he didn't want to get in the way, either. Torn, he stared after Officer Scanlon, who had already disappeared around the corner.

"Sir, I'd suggest that you take cover behind the car." Mark came up beside David as he, too, reached for his weapon. "This may be a false alarm, but it would be safer if you stayed out of the line of fire, just in case. We don't like to put civilians in danger. Back-up will be here in a couple of minutes."

Again, David hesitated. He wasn't a civilian. He was the man in love with the woman inside this building. And if this *wasn't* a false alarm, she was directly in the line of fire.

"Look, can I help in some way? I can't just hide behind…"

A woman's scream suddenly pierced the air from behind the building, followed by a gunshot. The surge of adrenaline that shot through David sent his pulse off the scale, and without waiting for Lowe to react, he turned and raced toward the alley.

"Hey! Not that way!" the man shouted.

Ignoring the warning, David plunged down the dark, narrow passage. A second later he heard the sound of running feet behind him.

When David emerged into the parking lot a couple of seconds later, the sight that met his eyes rocked the foundation of his world. Jared was on the ground, with Caroline kneeling beside him, holding his hand, while Scanlon trained his gun on two young thugs a short distance away. A knife lay on the ground beside them, and blood stained the pants of one of the punks at thigh level. The blood that caught—and held—David's attention, however, was on Caroline and Jared. Despite the deepening twilight, he could see that the lower part of Caroline's left arm was almost solid red. But the dark splotches on her green silk blouse were even more frightening. Jared's face was bloody, and there was a bright red stain on one side of his beige sport shirt.

Officer Lowe pushed past David, gun drawn, as he radioed for more back-up and an ambulance.

"Cuff them," Scanlon barked over his shoulder.

As Lowe complied, David's lungs kicked into gear again and he sprinted toward Caroline and Jared, dropping to one knee beside them. "Caroline?" His voice was so shaky he almost didn't recognize it.

She turned to him, dazed. One side of her face was as pale as a blank sheet of newsprint. The other was puffy and scraped raw, and there was a large, discolored lump on her temple. "David? Are you all right?"

His gut twisted. Despite her own injuries, her first worry was for him. "Yeah. But you're not."

"I—I'm okay. But Jared's hurt." The words came out choked and shaky as she transferred her attention back to the intern.

"You're not okay. Your arm is cut. Your face is swollen. There's blood on your blouse."

"The blood is from my arm. My face is fine. But they hurt Jared. They punched him, and kicked him in the ribs, and then they…they stabbed him in the side." Her voice broke, and her eyes filled with tears. "Please, David. Help him! Do something!"

Taking her assessment of her own condition at face value, David moved to Jared's other side. The boy looked up at him, his eyes glazed with pain, and when David took his hand, it was cold and clammy. Shock was setting in. Meaning he needed help. Fast. Just as David turned to call for assistance from the police, a sudden wail of sirens sent relief coursing through him. "Hang in there, Jared. Help will be here in a couple of minutes. Okay?"

"Yeah." The boy's voice was so soft it was almost inaudible.

David looked across Jared's prone form toward Caroline. The tears had spilled out of her eyes and begun to trickle down her cheeks as she focused on the boy, her face a mask of worry. She seemed oblivious to her own injuries, but David couldn't ignore her battered face or the blood that continued to ooze from a gash on her arm. Nor did he miss the limp hand that lay in her lap. He wouldn't rest easy until the paramedics had checked her out.

The tense wait seemed interminable, but finally help arrived. Within seconds, it seemed that cops were swarming all over the scene, and the paramedics went into action, easing David and Caroline aside as they bent over Jared. While Caroline recounted the attack on Jared and pointed out his injuries, David motioned to another paramedic. "She needs attention, too. Right away," he told the man, inclining his head toward Caroline.

"Okay." When Caroline finished discussing Jared, the EMT touched her shoulder. "Ma'am, let's move over to the side. I need to take a look at you."

Annoyed, she shook her head. "Later. I want to stay with Jared."

David stepped in. "*Now,* Caroline." He moved beside her and drew her to her feet with a firm hand.

Caroline opened her mouth to argue, but all at once her legs buckled and she sagged against David. He caught her, and before she realized his intent he reached down and tucked his arm beneath her knees, lifting her in one smooth motion.

"Where do you want her?" he asked the paramedic, his voice tight with tension.

"The stretcher over there." He pointed toward the ambulance.

As David strode toward it, Caroline spoke. "You're going to get blood on your suit. Put me down." She'd meant to sound forceful. Instead, her comment came out weak and shaky.

In any case, David ignored her. She had a good view of the solid set of his chin as he held her firmly against his chest, and she figured she might as well give up the fight. Besides, after the horror of the past twenty minutes, the haven of his arms felt good. And safe. And right.

"Right here, sir."

At the paramedic's instruction, David eased her down onto the stretcher. But he stayed close while the man checked her out. The EMT asked a series of questions as he worked to ensure he wasn't missing any serious injuries. He was joined a few minutes later by Officer Scanlon, who had his own set of questions. Caroline answered them all, and as she recounted the terrifying, violent experience she began to shake. David reached for her hand, enfolding it in a firm clasp as he turned to the policeman. "Can this wait until later? She's not up to all these questions right now."

"No problem. I just needed a few preliminaries."

"How's Jared?" Caroline turned to David as the officer left and the EMT cleaned the gash on her arm.

"I don't know."

"Can you find out?"

He didn't want to leave her. But he understood her concern. With a brief nod, he rose and made his way back to the paramedics clustered around the teen. "Can you tell me anything about his condition?"

One of the EMTs spoke without turning as he continued to work on Jared. "Stab wound. Appears to be superficial. Bruised nose. May be broken, but we won't know without X-rays. Possible broken ribs. Again, we need to confirm with X-rays. The preliminary prognosis looks good."

"Thanks."

By the time he returned to Caroline, the paramedic was just standing up, and David asked him the same question about her.

"Severe bruising on her face. The hospital will want to do some X-rays to check for a concussion and broken bones. The gash on her arm will require stitches. Looks like she has a sprained wrist. X-rays will confirm that, too. We're going to load her up now. Do you want to follow?"

"Yeah."

David dropped down to balance on the balls of his feet beside her. As he took her hand, her slightly unfocused eyes, shallow breathing and the strain around her mouth communicated her pain. His throat tightened, and when he spoke his voice was hoarse. "I'm going to follow you to the hospital, okay?"

"How's Jared?"

"It sounds like he'll be fine."

Relief eased some of the tension in her features. "Good."

The paramedics moved into position, and David leaned close. "I'll meet you at the hospital."

She tried to reach out to touch his face, wincing in pain at the effort.

Grasping her arm, he laid her hand gently on her chest and smoothed the hair back from her face. "Don't move, sweetheart."

"I was s-so afraid that y-you would walk into the middle of this and end up like M-Michael. I d-didn't want to lose you, too." Tears pooled in her eyes and her voice choked.

Once more his throat tightened with emotion, and he stroked her uninjured cheek. "I'm fine, Caroline. It's you I'm worried about."

"Sir, we need to get moving."

At the paramedic's voice, David rose and stepped aside. Weeks ago, he had acknowledged his love for this woman, who'd stolen his heart more than two years before. And he'd seen signs that she felt the same way. Yet she'd put up barriers—which wasn't surprising, considering all the baggage that came with their relationship. He hadn't pushed, believing that she'd let him know when the time was right. But tonight, in the midst of a narrowly averted tragedy, she'd given him a glimpse into her heart with that simple comment: "I didn't want to lose you, too."

And now that he knew her feelings paralleled his, it was time to take some action.

David pulled to a stop in front of Caroline's condo and wiped a weary hand down his face. Tonight had been a nightmare, but it was over. Caroline didn't have a concussion or any broken facial bones, the sprained wrist was mild and twenty-two stitches had taken care of the gash on her arm. Jared's ribs had been bruised again, but neither they nor his nose was broken. The puncture in his side had required some work, but it was a flesh wound and should heal with no complications. His grandmother and great-aunt had kept vigil with David and Caroline's mother until the wee hours, and now everyone was on their way home. No one was going to get much sleep this night, David realized, checking his watch. But at least they were all safe. When he thought about what could have happened... Sucking in a deep breath, he closed his eyes. *Thank You, Lord, for letting this end well.*

Looking over at his sleeping passenger, David's heart contracted with tenderness. From the first moment he'd seen her, David had been drawn to Caroline. Some instinct had told him that she was a one-in-a-million woman. Over the past few weeks, as he'd gotten to know her—and grown to love her—that initial impression had been confirmed over and over again. And he intended to tell her that as soon as possible. Not tonight, of course. But as soon as she was back on her feet.

"Sweetheart? You're home." He reached over and stroked the uninjured side of her face, which was closest to him.

Her eyelids flickered open, and for a second she seemed disoriented. Then, as her face cleared, she struggled to open her seat belt.

"Leave it." He stilled her hand with a touch. "I'll get it from the other side. Sit tight and I'll come around."

She didn't argue. She was too exhausted. Her face throbbed, her wrist ached and the numbing shots in her arm were wearing off. All she wanted to do was curl up in her bed and sleep for days.

A few seconds later, her door was pulled open. As David leaned across to unclasp her seat belt, taking care to avoid contact with her injured arm and face, her heart contracted with tenderness and gratitude. She wanted to reach out to him, to touch him, to ask him to hold her as he had done earlier in the evening. Not because she

was injured and hurting. But for different reasons
entirely. Except this wasn't the time, she realized, noting
the smudges beneath his eyes and the lines of worry
etched in his face. The night had been fraught with too
much emotional trauma already. They both needed to
get some rest.

Calling on every ounce of her strength, she swung her
legs to the ground and stood. David tucked an arm
around her waist as he pushed the door shut with his free
hand, and she leaned into him. She'd always prided
herself on being a woman who could stand on her own
two feet, but neither her feet—nor her legs—felt steady
enough to support her weight right now.

"Want me to carry you?" David murmured, his
worried voice close to her ear.

In truth, she did. But she shook her head. "I'll be
okay as long as I can lean on you."

"Anytime."

Their progress was slow, and negotiating the three
steps to her door taxed her energy to the limit. As if
sensing how close she was to collapse, David took the
key from her trembling fingers, inserted it in the lock
and guided her inside.

"Are you going to be okay here by yourself tonight?" he asked.

"The night's almost over."

"You know what I mean."

"Yeah. I do," she said softly. Although she'd been in
a lot of pain earlier, at the *Chronicle,* she hadn't missed
his murmured endearment then—or just now, in the car.
He'd called her sweetheart. And with that single word,

she'd known that his feelings for her ran deep and strong. Just as hers did for him. Now, as she looked at him, the banked fire in his deep brown eyes threatened to erupt into a consuming flame. But this man of discipline and self-restraint, this man of prudence, this man who always thought things through and seldom acted on impulse—this man she loved—managed to contain it. As if he, too, realized that now wasn't the time to explore their feelings for each other. "Will I see you tomorrow?" she asked.

A spark escaped from that contained fire, flaring with searing intensity for a brief second before it dimmed. "Count on it."

As she stood there, David reached over and touched her cheek. No words were spoken. None needed to be. Then he turned and walked to her door, pausing on the threshold before exiting for one more look that was loaded with meaning—and promise. And if Caroline's legs hadn't already been shaky, that look alone would have turned them to Jell-O.

David adjusted one of the red roses in the massive bouquet in his arms, then reached over and pushed Caroline's doorbell. He hoped he wasn't too early, but he'd stayed away as long as he could. What little sleep he'd managed had been fraught with nightmares of the possible tragic outcomes of last night's confrontation. Those heart-pounding dreams had wrenched him awake, adrenaline pumping, his breath lodged in his chest. He hoped Caroline had fared better.

But when she answered the door, he knew she hadn't.

There were dark circles under her eyes, and even though her cheek was no longer as puffy, a huge bruise, deep purple against her colorless skin, had replaced the redness. While she looked just as appealing in her cutoff shorts and T-shirt as she did in her usual chic, elegant wardrobe, her attire also revealed yet another large bruise, this one on her knee. Nevertheless, she managed a smile.

"I didn't expect you quite this soon. I thought you'd be at work. But those aren't your usual work clothes." She gave his worn jeans, which fit his lean hips like a second skin, and the sport shirt that hugged his broad chest a swift perusal.

"Not today."

"Well…come in." She stepped aside to let him enter, her stiff movements a clear indication of the physical trauma her body had endured. "How's Jared?"

"I talked to his grandmother this morning. He's doing okay. And I also talked to the police. The two punks who attacked you were happy to spill everything to save their own skin. They gave the police enough information to link the gang leaders to a couple of recent crime sprees and keep them off the streets for the foreseeable future. Without their leadership, the police think the gang will be history."

"I'm glad to hear that."

As she shut the door, David nodded to the crystal vase of flowers in his hands. "Where would you like these?"

"On the coffee table in the living room. Thank you. They're beautiful."

After depositing the flowers, he turned as she came up behind him. His compelling, intense eyes locked on hers, holding them captive as he took a step toward her, erasing the distance between them. When he was a whisper away, he reached up and brushed her hair back from her face, letting the silky strands glide through his fingers. Then, moving slowly—but with clear, deliberate intent—he leaned toward her and brushed his lips against hers in a brief kiss that was as light as a drifting leaf.

When she could find enough breath to speak, Caroline opened her eyes and stared at him. "I—I guess we have some things to talk about."

"I guess we do."

At the husky timbre of his voice, her heart stopped, then raced on. "Do you w-want to sit down?"

"Not really." He stroked a gentle finger down her cheek. "I want to kiss you again. I've been waiting to do that for…for a very long time. But I guess I can wait a few more minutes."

When she could drag her gaze away from his, she eased onto the couch. He sat beside her, angling his body to face her. "How about if I start?" he said.

Since she couldn't seem to find her voice, anyway, that sounded like a good plan, so she nodded.

Reaching out, he cradled her good hand in his, stroking the back of it with his thumbs as he spoke. "I have to be honest, Caroline. After I gave you the medallion, I never planned to see you again. I felt too guilty. You already know about the guilt I felt in connection with Michael's death. It took me a long time to work through that. What you didn't know about was the guilt I felt over my feelings for you." At her puzzled look, David drew a deep breath. "The fact is, you bowled me over the first time we met. And I couldn't get you out of my mind. Since you'd already given your heart to Michael, I tried my best to get over you. I told myself that what I felt for you was just infatuation. That in time it would fade. But the truth is, it never did. And once our paths started to cross again here in St. Louis, that original infatuation, or fascination, or obsession— or whatever it was—evolved into love. So my first instincts about you weren't that far off base after all."

A troubled look crossed his face, and David shook his head. "The thing is, I felt that my feelings for you were somehow wrong, even though Michael is gone. I struggled with that for a long time. Finally I talked it over with Steve, who helped me gain a little perspective. And to acknowledge something my heart has known with absolute certainty for a very long time— that all our tomorrows were meant to be spent together. He also helped me realize that if you felt the same way, I shouldn't let anything stand in the way of seeking out the love that the Lord seems to have guided us toward. Last Sunday in church, when you took off the medallion, I began to believe that maybe your feelings for me had evolved as well. That maybe, in time, you might come to love me—as I love you."

For most of their relationship, Caroline had sensed that David was a man of strong, but restrained, passion. A man able to mask what was in his heart, to maintain control of his emotions. She'd witnessed a few slight slips in the past several weeks. But nothing had prepared her for what she now saw. Gone were the barriers. Gone was the restraint. Gone was the mask. His eyes invited her to look deep into his heart. And the absolute love and devotion she saw there took her breath away.

Struggling to contain her tears of happiness, Caroline reached over and touched David's face. "I already do," she whispered.

Relief and thanksgiving and wonder washed over his face, intermingling, leaving joy in their wake.

"I know I should do this right…with candlelight and flowers and music…but after last night, I don't want to wait one more second. So…" He dropped to one knee and took her hands gently in his. "Would you do me the honor of becoming my wife?"

Her throat constricted with emotion, and she blinked back her tears. "I can't believe I've been blessed with a second chance for a happy ending."

"Is that a yes?"

A smile illuminated her face as she echoed his words from the night before. "Count on it."

At her positive response, a matching smile chased the anxiety from his features. "I'd like to seal this engagement with a proper kiss, but I think we'll have to be content with something simple until that bruise goes away." Regret tinged his voice as he surveyed her cheek.

"I'm a fast healer."

Her quick comeback brought a smile to his lips, and a chuckle rumbled deep in his chest. "That's good news. But in the meantime, let's try this on for size."

As he leaned close to claim her lips in a tender, careful kiss, Caroline closed her eyes, savoring the gift of love, of passage from winter to spring, that this special man had offered her. With him, and with trust in the

Lord, she'd found the courage to leave yesterday behind, embrace today and face tomorrow with joy. In other words, she was claiming the legacy Michael had left her by living the very philosophy that had guided his life.

And somehow, deep in her heart, she knew he would be pleased.

Epilogue

"I thought you were supposed to *cover* stories, not star in them."

Jared turned with a self-conscious grin toward Steve Dempsky, who was holding the latest issue of the *Chronicle*. Splashed across the front page was a feature article on the Uplink intern's recent first-place win in the national photography/journalism contest. "I'm kind of embarrassed by all the attention."

"Hey, enjoy the moment. It's not every day that a St. Louisan wins such a prestigious award. You deserve all the accolades you're getting."

"At least Nan seems proud. And Aunt Dara." He looked toward the two women, who were helping themselves to pizza and cookies from the long table in the *Chronicle*'s conference room.

"David told me you and your grandmother have moved in permanently with your great-aunt. How's that working out?"

"Great! The new school is cool. And they have an awesome photo studio." He looked around the room, then shook his head. "I still can't believe Ms. James went to all this effort for me after the trouble I caused." The entire *Chronicle* staff had been invited to the party celebrating Jared's win, along with his family, Charles Elliot and his former art and English teachers, and the Uplink board.

"She's one fine lady."

"Yeah." His grandmother motioned to him, and he waved back. "Excuse me. I need to see what Nan wants."

As Jared walked away, David joined Steve. "Hard to believe he's the same young man we interviewed, isn't it?"

"I'll say. But you had him pegged from the beginning. All he needed was a chance."

"And lots of TLC," Ella chimed in. She handed David a paper cup. "You forgot your punch."

"Thanks." He took it from her, then looked across the room to where Caroline was chatting with Bill Baker. Eight weeks after the attack, the bruises on her face had disappeared, the splint was off her wrist and a long-sleeved blouse hid the four-inch scar on her arm that would take a lot longer to fade. His gaze softened, and a smile touched the corners of his lips. "Caroline can take most of the credit for the TLC. She worked with him every day. I just provided moral support."

"Considering that rock on her finger, I think you provided a little more than that," Ella teased.

He turned to her. "Only after the fact. I don't mix business and pleasure."

"Honey, I'm not at all concerned about when. I'm

just glad it happened," Ella retorted with a grin. "You two were made for each other. Now I'm going to get me a piece of that pizza before this hungry horde devours every last scrap."

As Ella headed toward the table, intent on her purpose, Steve smiled at David. "She's right, you know."

Still focused on Caroline, David nodded. "Yeah. I know."

As if sensing his scrutiny, Caroline glanced his way. For a long second they just looked at each other. Then she turned back to Bill, said a few words and headed toward the two men.

"Uh-oh. Looks like my cue to exit," Steve remarked. "You know what they say about three being a crowd."

"You don't have to leave," David protested. "There's a whole roomful of people here."

"Maybe. But she only has eyes for you. And the reverse is true as well. Dinner next week?"

"It's on my calendar. See you then."

With a wave to Caroline, Steve sauntered away.

"I didn't meant to chase Steve off," she told David as she approached, a slight frown creasing her forehead.

Circling her waist with his arm, he pulled her close. "He left of his own accord. Mumbling something about three being a crowd."

"Should I go after him?"

His arm tightened. "Don't even think about it."

Smiling, she relaxed against him. "And you claim to be his friend."

"Hey, good friends know when to stick close—and when to get lost. Steve's a good friend."

She chuckled, then surveyed the room in satisfaction. "It's a nice party, isn't it? I think Jared was really touched."

"I know he was."

"He deserves it. That win is quite a coup for him. And for Uplink."

"I'm hoping it will smooth the way in the future for us to recruit kids like him. The ones who need us most."

"It can't hurt." Caroline let her head rest against David's shoulder as they watched the revelers. Jared's award-winning story and photos had been enlarged and were displayed on the one solid wall of the glassed-in conference room, and most of the guests were as impressed by the work as the contest judges had been. Although the internship had been fraught with difficulties, Caroline was glad she'd seen it through. In a way, she felt as if she'd paid back Michael's final debt, freeing her from any lingering guilt.

"What are you thinking?"

David's lips were close to her ear, his breath warm on her temple. She wanted to tell him, but she wasn't sure how to do it in a way that didn't sound like she was dwelling on the past. "About paying debts. And giving someone a chance," she replied softly. "And about moving on."

"I feel the same way."

Angling her head, she looked up at him. His eyes were warm and understanding, as if he could see right into her heart and knew exactly what she was feeling. That today, this moment, marked a turning point for them. It was as if they'd come to the end of the chapter in which Michael had played a major role, and tomorrow they would turn to a new, blank page waiting to be filled by the two of them.

Michael would always be a part of their lives, of course. But David sensed that the man they'd both loved would move away now as Steve just had, giving them the space they needed to create their own story. When Steve winked, grinned and gave a thumbs-up signal, David sensed another parallel, as well: that like Steve, Michael was smiling, too.

And as he rested his cheek against Caroline's silky hair, he gave thanks. For the woman he loved. For work that fulfilled him. For a faith that sustained and guided him. And for a brother who had taught him to see with fresh eyes—and to risk everything for the things that mattered most.

* * * * *

If you liked All Our Tomorrows, *be sure to look for Irene Hannon's next books,* The Family Man, *available in September 2006, and* Rainbow's End, *coming in January 2007, only from Love Inspired.*

Dear Reader,

As I write this letter, I am enjoying the end of spring, with my office window wide open. Air conditioning has not yet insulated me from the fresh scent of newly mown grass nor muted the song of the birds. I love this season, which has always represented hope and new life to me. It's a time to put the dark days of winter aside and step into the sunshine.

In *All Our Tomorrows,* Caroline and David learn to do just that with their lives. And as they leave the darkness of grief behind, step into the light of hope and embrace the promise of a new beginning, they trust that the Lord will lead and guide them on their journey together. I hope that their story uplifts and inspires you.

I'd also like to invite you to watch for my next book, *The Family Man,* which is the third book in the Love Inspired's Davis Landing series. This series debuts in July, and my book will appear in September. Although each book is a complete love story in itself, certain plot elements continue from one book to the next. I've never participated in a project like this before, which features a different author for each of the six books, but it promises to be a rewarding experience for me—and I hope for readers, as well!

Finally, I invite you to visit my Web site at www.irenehannon.com, where you can find news about my upcoming releases (not to mention scrumptious recipes!).

May you enjoy this season of sunshine, and may love grace your life this summer.

Irene Hannon

QUESTIONS FOR DISCUSSION

1. When David reappears in Caroline's life, she must reevaluate her negative opinion of him, which was based on secondhand information from his brother. Have you sometimes formed opinions about people—even judged them—based on others' interpretation and bias? Why is this dangerous—and unfair? What does the Bible tell us about judging others? Cite some instances from Scripture where the Lord speaks to this topic.

2. Distance insulated Michael from the harsh reality of his mother's condition. Nor did he seem to want to acknowledge it when informed. Can you think of any instances in your own life when you didn't want to face a difficult situation? Why not? How did your faith help you it address it?

3. As a youngster—and even into adulthood—David admired his outgoing older brother. But it can also be difficult to live in the shadow of a successful, popular sibling. Have you ever experienced this in your life? How has it affected your relationship with that sibling?

4. Following his mother's death, David reevaluates his life and takes a job where he hopes to improve lives, not just balance sheets. In explaining his decision to Caroline, he quotes Mother Teresa, "God has not called me to be successful, God has called me to be faithful." Why does it often seem difficult in today's society to follow this call?

5. In *All Our Tomorrows,* the Uplink board is nervous about reaching out to inner-city students like Jared. Yet David is convinced that those are the students most in need of the organization's assistance. All of us are faced with risky choices in our lives, choices that have great potential for good—but which can also backfire and do irreparable harm. Have you ever faced a situation like that? What did you do?

6. David and Caroline are struck by Jared's hope-filled photos. Why do you think Jared was able to hold on to hope despite his dismal surroundings? What role did his grandmother play in his attitude?

7. Jared pursues the Uplink internship despite the risks and threats. What gives him the courage to do so? How much impact did others' belief in him have on his willingness to persevere? Discuss examples from your own life where perseverance reaped positive results. How has your relationship with the Lord been a source of courage?

8. At first, Jared's grandmother is too proud to ask her sister for help when Jared needs a place to stay. Only when she realizes that asking for help is the best way to express her love, is she able to put her pride aside. What does the Bible tell us about the danger of pride? How can pride get in the way of our relationship with others—and the Lord?

9. A number of the characters have to deal with relationships gone awry. David and Michael experienced a rift; Jared's grandmother and her sister are estranged; Caroline and David start out on shaky ground because of resentments and misunderstandings. How might better communication have affected these relationships? What are some of the hallmarks of good communication?

10. In the end, both Caroline and Jared find their way back to God. Discuss their journeys and the factors that helped lead them home. Do any of their experiences parallel your faith journey?

2 Love Inspired novels and a mystery gift... Absolutely FREE!

Visit

www.LoveInspiredBooks.com

for your two FREE books, sent directly to you!

BONUS: Choose between regular print or our NEW larger print format!

There's no catch! You're under no obligation to buy anything. We charge nothing—ZERO—for your first shipment. And you don't have to make any minimum number of purchases.

You'll like the convenience of home delivery at our special discount prices, and you'll love your free subscription to Steeple Hill News, our members-only newsletter.

We hope that after receiving your free books, you'll want to remain a subscriber. But the choice is yours—to continue or cancel, anytime at all! So why not take us up on our invitation, with no risk of any kind!

TITLES AVAILABLE NEXT MONTH

Don't miss these four stories in August

MY SO-CALLED LOVE LIFE by Allie Pleiter
A special Steeple Hill Café novel in Love Inspired

Voicing a popular cartoon character hasn't been all fun and games for Lindy Edwards. And it's put a serious crimp in her love life. Now network consultant Leo Corbin is in town and his all-business attitude might spell the end for her beloved TV series. Could this grinch be a Prince Charming in disguise?

BY HER SIDE by Kathryn Springer
Davis Landing

When reporter Felicity Simmons received work-related threats, the Hamilton family turned to one of its own to protect her. Police officer Chris Hamilton pulled double duty investigating the threats and keeping Felicity safe, but never considered the real danger could be that Felicity would steal his heart.

IN HIS EYES by Gail Gaymer Martin

A decade ago, Ellene Bordini gave her heart to Connor Faraday and he broke it. Now he's back in town asking for a second chance. It wasn't hard for Ellene to fall for his young daughter, though forgiving Connor might take the biggest step of faith yet.

A SHELTERING HEART by Terri Reed

Gwen Yates was shocked when her boss made *her* the new leader for a mission trip to Africa…and added his handsome son to the expedition. Gwen promised she'd keep Derek busy, yet his masculine appeal might make that task more distracting than she anticipated.